CW00347297

Best wishes
Harry Lawrence

TEA, TRAITOR
and an MTB

BY

H.P. LAWRENCE

www.spinetinglerspublishing.com

Spinetinglers Publishing
22 Vestry Road, Co. Down
BT23 6HJ, UK
www.spinetinglerspublishing.com

First published by Spinetinglers Publishing, May 2011.

ISBN: 978-1-906755-14-0

Printed in the United Kingdom

This book is dedicated to the Isle of Wight Heart Care Club.

TEA, TRAITOR AND an MTB

THE BEGINNING
1942

Lt. Roger Carter RNVR arrived at Chatham docks just before 1400 hours, after a short train journey from London. He had had a meeting with Commodore Jones at the Admiralty.

"Just to let you know, Carter, you will be carrying an extra passenger tonight, a Major Ambrose Cummings. He is one of those intelligence chaps."

The Commodore walked over to the window, a look on his face that made you think something was worrying him.

"Major Cummings will meet you at Chatham docks. He will be in the NAFFI waiting for you."

Commodore Jones sat back at his desk, sorted some paperwork, then told Carter that tonight he would be doing a routine patrol with three other MTBs, under command of Lt. Slater. Intelligence had informed them that there was a convoy of six merchant vessels escorted by three armed trawlers, leaving Ostend for Norway. He would lay off and wait for the convoy. Once sighted, the other three MTBs would attack. Carter would leave them and make for Salsouse, just north of Dunkirk, where he would drop off Major Cummings, and then rejoin the others.

"Is there any opposition about — you seem a little worried — is there anything else I should know?" Carter asked.

"Not according to Cummings, but he will fill you in on any detail you want. Just drop him off and get away. I'm not keen on all this but orders are orders. I don't like the idea of someone going into an enemy held country with knowledge of all our agents in Belgium and Holland."

"What would he be doing in those countries?" said Carter.

"Major Cummings has come up with an idea of getting all the agents to report to a central control rather than all trying to get through to England, hopefully to stop messages back and forth by everyone."

"How many agents are we talking about? I get the feeling you are not keen on Major Cummings," replied Carter.

The Commodore said he thought about twenty agents and intimated that Cummings had an aura about him that made the Commodore distrust him.

* * *

Carter was still pondering the situation when the guard at Chatham asked for his pass. He then made his way to MTB 265, to be greeted by his number one, *Junior* as he was called, due to his having the same name as the units' commander, Tom Brown.

He informed Junior of the guest on board for this trip, a Major Cummings of Army Intelligence.

"Nice one, Skipper. I'll stow his gear in the mess. Not much room elsewhere."

Carter explained there wouldn't be much luggage as it was a one way trip, and he would go to the NAAFI to collect the Major ready for the 2000 hr briefing alongside. Lt Slater and the three other boats would sail at 2130 hrs.

* * *

Carter entered the NAAFI that was busy with boat crews. Looking around he saw an army major talking to some seamen.

"Major Cummings?" Carter asked.

"Yes. You must be Lieutenant Carter."

"If you have finished?" Carter answered curtly. "We can get aboard. I have some paperwork to do."

"Right. I've just been talking to some sailors. They don't get a lot of rest between duties."

"They should not be talking about what they do," Carter said with a curious look.

"I am an intelligence officer," explained Cummings.

Carter said no more as they made for MTB265. Junior was waiting at the bow, Major Cummings said he would carry his small case and that as he was only going one way he carried little.

* * *

Carter soon shouted down from the chart room, "Briefing in 10 minutes!"

Alfred, the port side gunner and mess orderly made sandwiches and a hot brew, which was welcomed by all.

Carter began, "We have Major Cummings with us this

trip, our orders are to keep with the other boats until they sight the convoy. Once sighted we will leave them and make for Salsouse where we will drop Major Cummings off. Then we will rejoin the others attacking the small convoy which is escorted by three armed trawlers bound for Norway"

Junior opened the chart of the North Sea showing the Belgian and Dutch coast. The crew gathered around.

"I'm informed by Major Cummings that the small village of Salsouse is quiet — no known troops as they are further along the coast, so should be a quiet run in. There is a small jetty which we will use."

2130 hours: The four craft under command of Lt Slater RN eased out of Chatham and were soon through the Thames defences and heading out into the North Sea.

Lt Slater joined the RN in 1936, spending most of the time in cruisers, but when the call came for young men to volunteer for MTBs and gun boats, he was one of the first to apply.

"Signal from lead boat sir, 'Follow me'."

"Acknowledge, Junior," said Carter.

Speed increased as darkness fell. It was a cloudy, overcast night with a chance of rain.

About two thirds across the North Sea Lt Slater slowed and signalled for silent running, with engines just ticking over.

0200 hours: The lead boat signalled, "Convoy sighted. Follow me. Good luck Carter."

The three MTBs sped off and Carter turned onto a new heading for Salsouse.

Major Cummings came onto the bridge with his gear. He had changed into civvies "When we get close I'll signal to make sure it's all clear. I have a friend waiting."

Carter could just make out the coast line with a small jetty. He told Davies to make for this and to keep it on his port side, making it easier to get ashore.

Cox'n Davies acknowledged. He was an old hand serving on North Sea trawlers and his duties were second nature to him.

Major Cummings sent four short flashes towards the jetty. A little while later five flashes came back.

"That's the signal, all is okay," Cummings said.

"We will go straight in, unload quickly and away," Carter replied.

MTB265 eased its way alongside the jetty. Two seamen jumped ashore and took the lines, keeping hold of them ready for letting go.

Cummings put his gear on the jetty and turned to Carter. "Just one thing I've not told you. I have a good position waiting for me in Berlin."

At that moment gunfire came from all directions. German troops were running along the jetty. It was all over in seconds.

Carter was still alive and saw Cummings coming over to him.

"Bad luck Carter. Your boat will be towed out among the rocks and sunk, never to be found."

Carter felt a bang on his head and a falling sensation; he had been pushed down the forward hatch into the cable locker.

CHAPTER 1

1999

Joanne woke suddenly by the violent movement of her boat. She rushed up to the wheelhouse.

"Who are you and what are you doing on my boat?" she shouted.

"I don't really know, but if I could start this boat we might not run into those rocks."

Joanne lifted a flap below the control panel and got out some keys.

"If you don't mind, I'll take over now." With that the powerful engine bust into life and was soon clear of the rocks.

"So how did you get on my boat? That uniform looks a bit dated."

"My name is Lieutenant Roger Carter RNVR. My boat was sunk among those rocks; your anchor broke loose and hooked on my cable locker pulling it off. The next minute I was on your boat"

"What are you trying to say, you were in the cable locker?" Joanne looked a little worried at this point.

"Auntie Joanne, who you talking to?" asked a young girl

6

coming onto the bridge.

"This man here" Joanne said.

"What man where?" asked Karen.

"Can't you see him?" answered Joanne.

"No one there Auntie."

Joanne looked at Carter. "Why can't she see you?"

"I don't know. Maybe I'm a ghost. You saw me because you expected to see someone."

"Okay, this has gone far enough. Get off my boat" Joanne said, pointing over the side.

"This is an odd looking boat. What's it made of?" Carter asked, taking no notice of what was said.

"It's GRP glass reinforced plastic."

"When was it built?"

"Nineteen ninety-four at Poole in Dorset."

"So what year are we in now?"

"Nineteen ninety-nine," said Joanne. "Don't you know anything?"

"Who won the war? I've been down below for fifty-seven years then."

"We won," answered Joanne.

"Auntie, you are talking to yourself again."

"Karen, I'll explain later. Go and make me a cup of coffee, please."

"Tell me what happened to you?" asked Joanne.

Carter began to explain how his boat MTB265 was going to Salsouse to drop off an agent who turned out to be a traitor, and how they were met by German soldiers who killed all his crew. "This traitor banged me on the head and put me down the cable locker, they then towed my boat out to the rocks and sank her, where I stayed until you released me."

"So you don't know what happened to the traitor?"

asked Joanne.

"I've no idea. Last he said was he was going to have a good job in Berlin, and later when Germany won the war a better job in England."

"What was his name?

"Major Ambrose Cummings," said Carter

"There is a Lord Ambrose Cummings; he is president of the Prisoner of War Association."

"So he is still alive. Where does he live?" Carter asked with a frown on his face.

"I think he lives near Cambridge. He has an office there," said Joanne. "He will be getting old now, do you think that it's the same man?"

"You must get me back to England; I'll find out all right, but not sure what I can do about it."

"Lord Cummings is a highly respected and decorated person, often on TV at remembrance services. He was a prisoner of war and helped many escape," Joanne replied.

"Where do you come from?" asked Carter.

"I'll be going back to Chatham. That's where I keep the boat," Joanne answered.

"That's very handy. That's where I was based — Chatham docks, Number Three Pontoon" said Carter.

"My father worked at Chatham docks during the war. He lives just around the corner from the dock gates."

Karen bought a mug of tea for Joanne and two biscuits. "One for you and one for your friend," she said laughingly.

"Very funny, Karen," said Joanne.

"Shall I make her jump or something?" Carter said softly to Joanne.

Joanne just smiled, wondering how long Karen would be amused by the new "friend."

8

They were making good time and soon entered the Thames estuary.

"Are you sure nobody can see you?" asked Joanne as she radioed to report her return.

"I don't know. It's a first for me, but I don't think so."

While Karen was on the bridge Joanne decided not to talk to Carter, thinking she would let time decide if and when, if Karen saw Carter then she would tell her.

* * *

The entrance to Chatham docks was very busy. Joanne turned to Karen. "I think we will wait until it gets quieter, as there's not much room on my pontoon."

They waited and then Carter came close to Joanne and said could he take the boat in, Joanne commented it had been 57 years since Carter had handled a boat, but Carter said he felt as though it was yesterday. He proceeded to take over the controls and eased the boat onto its moorings. When Carter touched the throttle, his hand touched Joanne and she shivered.

Karen jumped ashore securing the head rope as Joanne followed with the stern line.

Karen then sorted the springs and fenders while Joanne turned off the engine.

"I hope nobody saw that," said Joanne

"I think you came alongside very nicely," Carter said jokingly.

Karen came back on board. "How did you do that Auntie? Your hand hardly touched the wheel or the throttle. I was watching you."

"I decided to take a chance and it worked," Joanne answered. "And before we go home come below. I think there's something you should know."

They went below into the galley where Joanne started making tea. "Karen, when we dragged our anchor at Salsouse it got caught on a sunken boat."

Joanne told the story so far. "So if you believe, look carefully to your left. Can you see a man in navel uniform sitting next to you?"

Karen jumped. "Something is happening — I saw a face."

"Believe in the face and you will see a Lieutenant Roger Carter RNVR."

"Hello, Karen, I'm Roger."

Karen mumbled a hello, still feeling very nervous.

After all was settled Joanne said it was time to go home, telling Carter that he had better stay on the boat. She would check her laptop for any more information about Ambrose Cummings, and she would be back in the morning.

After 10 minutes of explaining what a laptop was, and showing Carter its basic use, Joanne and Karen left.

CHAPTER 2

Joanne could not sleep much that night, trying to take it all in.

Karen also was up most of the night. She made Joanne a hot drink and they sat on the bed talking things over. The next morning she rang her father, asking if he could remember an MTB Flotilla based at Chatham Docks during the war.

Joanne's father, Derek, said there were two flotillas at Chatham plus one gunboat flotilla. One would go out one night, the other the next night unless things got busy. Then all would go out together.

"I have some photos of some of the boats and crews. Why so much interest?"

"A little project I'm doing. Do you remember things quite well?"

"Oh yes. I remember one cheerful chap, name of Junior, always trying to get extra rations from the stores. Sometimes I would give him some extras."

* * *

Joanne and Karen arrived at her father's house within half

an hour, eager to see the photographs.

Joanne's father got out an old biscuit tin from the cupboard under the stairs. "Should be in here. Ah yes, here they are." Derek laid six photos on the table.

Joanne looked at them. The fourth one made her go white.

"Are you all right?" asked Derek.

"Do you know who these people are in this photo alongside MTB265?" asked Joanne.

"That's the young man I was telling you about, went by the name of Junior."

"Who is that one?" Joanne asked.

"That's Lieutenant Carter. He was the skipper — one of the finest he was. They went out one night with other boats but never came back. Why the interest?" asked Derek.

"Can I have this photo, Dad?"

"Yes, of course, you can take the lot. I'm sure you will tell me what you're up to in due course."

Karen looked at the photo. "That's the man on your boat," she said.

"What man on your boat? asked Derek.

"Dad, if I tell you a story, don't get excited. Remember your heart."

Joanne began telling her father what had happened the day before. Derek asked Joanne if Lord Cummings was a traitor, how come he had helped prisoners of war? He was eager to meet Lt Carter — he had admired him so much.

Joanne said she would arrange a meeting later, but first she needed to know how to check out the concerns about the Major. "See you later Dad," said Joanne as she put the photos in her bag. Joanne and Karen left, and made straight for her boat.

* * *

"That was a nice bit of seamanship yesterday coming alongside. A pity more cannot handle a boat like that," said old Tom. He was always fishing off one of the Pontoons and usually noticed much of the comings and goings.

"Did you like it?" replied Joanne. She looked towards Karen and they both grinned.

Karen climbed aboard the boat warily and called out to Roger.

"I'm here," said a voice from below.

Joanne entered the lounge, eager to show Carter the photographs.

"Did you sleep last night, or don't you sleep?" asked Karen.

"I did sleep. I seem to turn off after a while, and need to recharge myself."

"Take a look at these photos," Joanne said placing them on the table. "Is that you — and who is that one?"

"Yes. That's me, and that is Junior with the rest of my crew."

Joanne told Carter that her father took the photos as he worked at Chatham Docks Quartermaster stores until he retired.

Roger looked again and recalled a young Derek Kilmore in the stores. He remembered the picture being taken just after he took command of MTB265.

Joanne started to tell Carter that her father knew someone that used to be in naval intelligence during the war, and he might know who could help him.

"I don't think I'm in a position to go around seeing people, but if you could arrange a meeting with this man I could be beside you and prompt you."

With only two weeks of her holiday left, Joanne was eager to start digging into the story; she opened her mobile phone and called her Dad.

Carter just stood in amazement. To see the mobile phone and now the laptop being expertly used fascinated him, he wondered what else the 57 years had brought in progress. His few minutes watching the laptop work had left his enquiring mind longing for more, but he patiently watched Joanne looking up Major Cummings to see if he and Lord Cummings were one and the same man.

"Here we are, is that your Major Cummings?" she asked Carter, showing him the photo on her laptop.

Carter took no time in saying, "That's him all right. I'll never forget that face. Older or not, he still has that sideward grin."

He began reading that Lord Ambrose Cummings, Director of Prisoners of War Association, was an ex-prisoner himself who helped many other prisoners to escape. He spent the last years of the war in Colditz, before escaping himself, just as the British began to gain entry to Colditz.

Major Cummings became a politician after the war, then campaigned for ex-prisoners of war to be recognised. He retired from politics in 1982 to concentrate on the POW Association and in 1993 was made Lord Cummings and Director of the Association.

Joanne turned to Carter who was leaning on the side of the boat and asked if he had heard what she had read.

"Yes," said Carter, "but it makes me feel so angry. I'm getting tired I need a rest — I'm beginning to fade." With that Carter slowly went.

A minute later Joanne received the news she needed, that

her father's friend would see her and check out feasibility of her story. She asked when and where and looked again at Carter, asking him if he was able to concentrate.

"I'm beginning to wake up. I wish I knew why I keep getting tired. I expect it's because I'm not really supposed to be here," Carter replied. He was thrilled that Joanne had believed him and would help him.

"Yes. In for a penny, in for a pound, as Dad would say."

The mobile rang again and Derek said how intrigued his friend was and he looked forward to seeing them the next day at 2 pm.

"Cuppa, Auntie?" Karen shouted from below. "I've given you two long enough, now count me in whatever you intend doing. Remember I'm fourteen now and want to help."

CHAPTER 3

Carter looked at the BMW parked outside Joanne's house, noting it was German. 57 years ago there was a war on and no one would have a German car. One hundred twenty mph and comfort came with the times now.

They soon arrived at a cottage on the outskirts of Tunbridge Wells, and were met by a big man with an Irish setter.

"Hello, I'm Stephen Harris; let us see if I can help you."

They entered into a large lounge, full of old memorabilia.

As tea and coffee was being poured, Joanne noticed the dog sniffing around where Carter was standing and she glanced at Karen and grinned.

Joanne told Stephen the story so far, and wondered if he knew anybody who might help and look into the accusations.

While this was going on Carter was looking at the bookcase full of books entitled World War II, thinking he would like to read them.

Stephen thought for a moment. "Can you think of anything that might help me believe you? Anything about Cummings for example? Ask your friend some personal detail."

"Ask him yourself," said Joanne. "He's here next to me."

"Really?" said Stephen. "I'm not usually known for talking to empty spaces, so I'll let you ask."

Joanne asked Carter, who said he only knew Cummings for a short while and all he remembered was his sideways smirk.

Stephen remembered that grin very well from seeing TV interviews, making Cummings look almost idiotic. He offered to put Joanne in touch with a man in the Navy, who also worked for MI5, being the son of Stephen's brother he knew he would listen, being a dab hand at unusual cases.

Joanne thanked him profusely and promised to send kind regards to her father. Once in the car she rang him and told him of being able to meet Tim Harris.

"Stephen's nephew," remarked Joanne's father. "Know him very well, he went to the same collage as you He's about two years older."

"Can't place the name. Anyway, I'm seeing him tomorrow afternoon. See you later Dad, and thanks."

* * *

Carter marvelled at the mobile phone, itching to send messages. "You will have to show me how that works one day," he said. "But for now could you drop me off at your boat? I'm very tired."

Back at Joanne's house with Karen they both sat down and began to write everything that had happened since the first meeting with Carter.

"What if this Tim Harris doesn't believe us?" asked Karen, picking up the photo of Carter and his crew. "They were all young men, and he still looks the same, uniform

17

and all."

"I don't know, but we can't do anything on our own. Lord Cummings is quite a well-known person. I just hope we get a favourable outcome tomorrow — a busy day ahead methinks."

CHAPTER 4

Joanne woke with a start. It was just getting light, and the rain was quite heavy. She quietly made tea and toast, and then woke Karen. They were both concerned about getting involved, but they knew Carter was relying on them.

"I'll drop you off first Karen, then pick up Carter. Your dad should be home by now." Joanne smiled fondly at the teenager and then promised to recall the day's events to her later. Hopefully Tim Harris would be a great help today.

Arriving at her boat, Joanne found Carter looking at a book on radar.

"Good morning," she said. "How are you this morning?"

"I didn't get any rest — kept worrying about today. I've been reading this book on radar. It's come a long way since the ones I've seen."

"Are you sure you will be okay? It could be a tiring day."

"I'm ready. Let's get started. I want to get this done," Carter said in a firm voice.

* * *

The journey to London was hectic and took a long time. As

19

they finally arrived at MI5 Carter sat and marvelled at the cars and buses and how crowded it was, the new buildings with all glass fronts, and how the world really had moved on.

After all the signing in and inspections she was shown to an interview room where a middle- aged woman asked her to sit and would she like tea or coffee. "If you want to hang up your coat Lieutenant Harris will be with you shortly."

Just then a young man in naval uniform entered and introduced himself as Tim Harris.

"Hello," said Joanne as she watched Harris start writing.

"First things first — name, address, phone number." Then he asked for the story.

Joanne once again told what she knew to date, while this was going on Harris kept looking at the other chair beside Joanne, all the time making notes.

"Tell me, Miss Kilmore, is your friend Carter with you now?

"Yes and he can hear every word you say," Joanne answered.

"That's probably why I can feel a presence here," remarked Harris. "This is why you are seeing me. I deal with unusual cases."

"You do?" said Joanne, surprised. "Good; then maybe you will believe me, and please call me Joanne."

There was a tap on the door. "Enter," said Harris.

A woman with a tray came in. "Tea and biscuits, Mr Harris," she said.

"Thank you, Ann," replied Harris. Turning to Joanne he said, "I'll get all the records I can on Lord Cummings and will be in touch sometime tomorrow. Also, I can find out what happened to MTB265."

"Thank you for listening to me. It's not a pleasant story," Joanne said, putting on her coat.

"If true, it is very disturbing," Harris answered.

"It's all true," Carter said to Joanne. "Ask him what happened to all the agents that Cummings had a list of in Belgium and Holland."

"Carter asks what happened to the agents in Belgium and Holland at that time."

Harris made some more notes. "Right. I've got that, thank you again. I'll contact you tomorrow. Goodbye Joanne, and good day to you, Lieutenant Carter."

Ann came into the office, she and Harris looked out of the window at Joanne in the car park. "If this is true, it's a big problem for the government," Harris said.

"And the British Legion. I'll get onto this straight away," leaving Harris with his thoughts as she picked up her notes.

* * *

Outside Joanne sighed. She was pleased that Tim Harris seemed interested and looked forward to his findings. Before getting into her car Joanne rang Karen and explained what had happened.

Arriving back at her boat Joanne asked Carter if he was OK.

"Just a little tired. I can't stay awake too long. Let's hope Lieutenant Harris finds something. Otherwise I don't know what to do."

"I think he more than half believed me. Tomorrow morning I'll go and see my father; perhaps the day after you would like to visit him, too."

"I'd like that," said Carter and wished her a good night.

21

Joanne phoned her father and told him all that had happened, and that Carter will be coming to see him the day after tomorrow. She suggested that he write down anything he remembered of when Lt Roger Carter left Chatham in charge of his MTB.

CHAPTER 5

Joanne woke at 6 am and made a mug of tea. She found the tin with the photos and started browsing through them again, hoping to pick out new points. Greeting her father later Joanne said she had been musing on the way life had been back in the war years.

"Not good times — air raids all the time, boats being loaded for the night run, docks being bombed, everything on ration. No, not good times." said Derek.

"What was Lieutenant Carter like as a person?" asked Joanne.

"Can't remember a lot. The whole family came from Jersey, just before the Channel Isles fell into German hands. Carter and his brother were in the RNVR, his father was a Lieutenant Commander and head of the Channel Isle RNVR. They came to England with other members in their unit's patrol craft. There was also a sister."

"What happened to his family?"

"His brother was posted to Shoreham on gun boats — no idea what happened to him after that."

"What about his sister and mother?" Joanne asked.

"The sister's name was Maria — married a chap also on MTBs — and can't remember his name. I don't think the

23

Mother came to England. The father was an artist who went to France and disappeared undercover."

Joanne said she had better get going, and asked if she could bring Carter along tomorrow.

"Please, I would like to meet him again" said her father.

* * *

The next day Carter was sitting in the wheelhouse when Joanne arrived, she asked how he felt. Carter seemed to be getting more tired each day and he hoped he could stay awake. Joanne told him of more unearthed photographs and Carter was eager to see them and her father again.

"Sounds great, be nice to see him too. We could talk about how the world has changed."

Joanne had rung Karen and arranged to pick her up. "Back seat, Karen we have a guest with us."

Karen then saw Carter, who on greeting her made her jump.

"Hello," said Karen. "I can see you better today."

They arrived at Joanne's father's house where Derek greeted them. "Come on in, have you had breakfast"

Joanne replied they could do with a drink but were eager to get on. "Dad, this is Lieutenant Carter."

"Hello, Lieutenant Carter, it's been a long time."

"Not for me," said Carter.

Joanne repeated it to her father.

"No, I guess not. I've got some more photos Carter might like to look at."

After a cup of tea, Derek suggested that Joanne and Karen might like to go somewhere. Carter could stay behind and the two men could discuss the years gone by.

Karen and Joanne wanted to go to Cambridge and see

24

where Lord Cummings lived. Carter and Derek Kilmore begged them to be careful, but they assured him they were just going to look, not to see Lord Cummings.

Derek couldn't see Carter but knew he was there; he emptied the tin of photos on the table. "Have a look at those while I get some World War Two books for you to look at."

Carter studied the photos. One in particular he remembered being taken, and it was only eight days ago in his time.

Derek came back with some books. "This should keep us busy for a while. If you want any more information give me a sign or something."

Lt Carter was soon engrossed in reading what had happened after his demise.

* * *

Joanne and Karen made good time driving to Cambridge, and they headed straight for the library. Joanne asked at the reception which road to take to get to Lord Cummings' house, and if they had any information leaflets regarding Lord Cummings, as she wanted to write an article in a magazine.

After directions Joanne and Karen set off, remembering to turn left at the junction with a supermarket on the right hand side. Karen was looking at the leaflet advertising the POW aux fund, and found an address for the Cambridge office of their Director, Lord Cummings. About half a mile along the road they spotted a big wide gate with a brass plate announcing Lord Cummings' residence. Turning round they decided that the house was a very expensive one and thought they would check out his office too.

They parked the car in a car park near the centre of town, and walked towards the High Street. "Excuse me, could you tell me where Turner Avenue is?" Joanne asked a passer-by.

"Yes. Just turn right, and then second on the left."

Joanne thanked him and was soon looking at number 11.

"Do you think we should go in?" she asked Karen. While they were making up their minds a Jaguar car pulled up and out stepped Lord Cummings. He went straight into the office.

"I think at the moment we go back and have a look at his house. We know he's not home," Karen suggested.

Parking back from the house, they walked up the narrow road until the big gates were in sight. There was a high wall with wire on top, and Karen noticed some cameras, one by the gate and another along the wall.

"Not taking any chances," said Joanne. "Let's just look like bird watchers."

They got back to the car and headed back to Joanne's father's house, satisfied that they had seen Lord Cummings.

* * *

"Had a good day, Dad?" asked Joanne. "How did you and Carter get on?"

"I think it went okay. I did all the talking, but had the feeling I was not alone."

Carter moved close to Joanne. "Tell your father I enjoyed it very much and would like to do it again soon. I was very interested in how man got on the moon, and all the new bombs — very interesting indeed."

When these words were repeated to Derek he smiled and

26

replied, "Good, anytime but meanwhile let's hope Carter gets things sorted and finally gets some peace."

Karen was eager to get going from her granddad's house that day; a treat would be staying with Joanne and talking to Lt Carter on the way.

Joanne told Carter what had happened, how they had seen Cummings and looked at his house.

Carter expressed a wish to see inside the Major's home and Joanne thought that the week-end might be a better time to catch him at home.

Leaving Carter at the boat, and telling him they would be back in the morning, Joanne and Karen set off for home.

After a hot chocolate they both settled down to discuss the day's events.

CHAPTER 6

Ann arrived at the Ministry of Defence early, as she wanted to do a lot of research and knew that MOD records department always took a long time, as the paperwork involved could never be rushed. She often thought they only employed people with one speed, slow. Not really true of course, it just seemed that way.

Piles of the records of Allied agents in Belgium and Holland between 1940 and 1944 eventually were carefully placed at a desk and after two hours she found one marked "Allied agents missing, captured, or killed, 1939 to 1945."

Ann was about to ask if she could have a copy of the file when a security guard told her that the building closed in two minutes for lunch, and reopened at 1400 hours.

She went back to MI5 and told Tim Harris what she had found.

Tim had a good look at her notes. "I think we will continue with this. I wonder how we can get the list of agents that Cummings had."

"There must be some record at the Admiralty. I'll give my friend a ring, and let's hope they can find a list of agents who were operating in Belgium and Holland."

28

* * *

Lt Brendan Parker, RN, entered Tim's office with Ann.

"Hello Tim. I've bought as much as I could find on agents at that time. I don't know what happened to most of them, only the ones the Navy took over. What's this all about?"

Tim looked at the file while Ann explained what they were looking into.

He read that a sudden purge during 1942-44 by the Germans against agents in Belgium and Holland resulted in most being shot or captured, and then after 1944 most survived. He told them they must get a copy of the file from the MOD, as that might enlighten them. Lt Parker had been assigned to help them too, which pleased Tim Harris who welcomed him to the world of mystery.

"Ann can get Parker up to speed, and obtain the file copy. I want to see Joanne Kilmore again, and try and get any more info."

Telephoning Derek he found that she was at her boat with Karen. Her Dad confided he was glad Harris was looking into it as he didn't want Joanne getting hurt or fobbed off .

Tim said he quite understood and would be sorting this out one way or another, it made a change to get his teeth into something different.

* * *

Harris reached the boat after battling the rush hour traffic. "Hello Joanne, I thought I would come and see you on your own ground. It can be a little uneasy at MI5."

"Welcome aboard," said Karen. "Tea or coffee — I

presume you have not come on a social call?"

"Tea, please. Joanne, do you have any more information that might help?"

"Say hello to Lieutenant Carter," said Joanne, pointing to the helm where Carter was sitting.

"Hello, Lieutenant Carter. I hope you can hear me and understand me."

"He understands okay," said Joanne.

Harris explained there was a list of agents that were captured or killed during '42 and '44 and what they were looking at now was trying to match those names with the list that Cummings had.

"Carter says he never saw any list. It was mentioned to him by Commodore Jones at the briefing. He said, "It was Cumming's idea to get all agents in those areas to report to a central control."

"Right, it's unfortunate Commodore Jones died in 1962," Harris answered.

Carter thought somehow the Commodore must have had a signal to have mentioned it.

"I'll check that out tomorrow." Harris scribbled on a pad. "What I also want is the exact location of MTB265. Could you get the Lat. and Long. from your chart?"

Joanne took two minutes to check her chart and then gave Harris the Lat. and Long.

"Good, what I'm going to do is to get my friends in the Dutch Navy to try and locate the wreck. If found I will put an advertisement in all British Legion magazines, and see what happens, then contact Lord Cummings' office casually saying, 'Good news, have you heard the Dutch Navy have found MTB265? That's the boat you were on before it was attacked, thought you might want to know.'"

"Let's hope there is some sort of reaction," said Joanne."

"Right. I'll leave you now. I will keep you informed on anything that happens."

Harris left while Joanne, Karen and Carter pondered over what he had said.

CHAPTER 7

Lt Parker entered the Admiralty and made straight for the press room. He asked for a release to all magazines and papers going to press that week, stating he would be giving the full story and a photo later. "There is a tight time limit for entries in the next editions," remarked a rating.

Parker assured him that it would be authorised from the top so there was no worry.

Meanwhile, Harris contacted the Dutch Navy who were only too glad to search for MTB265, and would let Harris know any outcome.

Back at the MOD Ann also was busy, looking for any records of Lord Cummings' being in any POW camps, and any other prisoners who might have come in contact with him, she came across names and addresses of four Colditz POW who now lived in London.

Ann phoned Harris. "There are two who live close, I'll pop around and have a word." Harris agreed that was a good idea, and asked Ann to ascertain if anyone remembered seeing Cummings in any camp.

* * *

Ann soon arrived at the first address. "Hello, Mr Wears, my name is Ann. I'm from MI5,"she said, showing her ID, "could I have a moment of your time?"

"Come in, I don't get many visitors. Would you like a cup of tea?"

Ann asked if she could help. "No, it's okay. I was about to have one when you came."

"Mr Wears, I understand you were in Colditz?"

"Yes, from 1942 to 1945, when the British arrived"

"Can you recall ever coming across a Major Cummings?"

"Is that the Lord Cummings?" asked Wears. "Never came across him at Colditz. I was a member of the escape committee, but there were prisoners coming and going constantly."

Ann thanked him for his help and making for the door said she would get in touch again sometime.

Mr Wears suddenly remembered a man called Tom Dermont who lived nearby and told Ann he had kept a diary at Colditz. Ann quickly wrote down the address of Blake Rest Home, part of the British Legion. Mr Wears told her he would telephone Tom Dermont.

After about two minutes explanation to Tom Dermont, Wears said, "If we go now he can see us before dinner, because after that he falls asleep."

* * *

Arriving at the rest home they were shown into a big lounge. Wears walked straight over to Tom, "Hello, Tom. I have a friend who would like to ask you a few questions about Colditz."

"Hello, Tom, my name is Ann. I come from the Admiralty. I understand you used to keep a book on comings and goings at Colditz."

"That's right. It was meant to be a record of all British prisoners, more like a ledger."

"What happened to it after the war?" Ann asked.

"Don't really know. I did hear something about going to the Ex POW Association."

"Tom, can you remember a Major Ambrose Cummings being a prisoner?"

Tom took a long time to answer. "Don't recall writing that name but my memory is getting a little confused these days. I do remember bringing it up a few years ago when Lord Cummings was made Director of the Ex POW Association. He said he helped prisoners escape. At the meetings we would often joke saying where from? Why the interest – is something wrong?"

Ann reassured him that it was nothing that should worry him and thanked him for his time, promising at the same time to let Mr Wears know the outcome.

Ann sat in her car for another twenty minutes writing down all that was said, then she made her way back to HQ.

* * *

Harris was eager to hear how she had got on that day and Ann passed over the notes she had made.

Parker, meanwhile, was trying to find any information about the other MTBs that went out that night, and if Lt Slater was still around. He was told he lived with his daughter in Brighton. "Do you want his address? Sorry, don't have a phone number," said the voice on the phone.

"Thanks Matthew, I owe you one," replied Parker.

Harris, Parker and Ann sat around the desk with bits of

paper everywhere.

"There seems to be something not quite right," said Harris

"On face value Lord Cummings does not add up," remarked Parker.

"I think we have a lot of work to do. Dig deep into files, if Ann's contacts ever heard of him in any POW camps."

Harris opened his flip chart and said that they would start making a profile; Ann would go to the British Legion and make enquiries; Parker would go to Brighton and see Lt Slater to ask if he had any thoughts on what happened that fateful night.

* * *

Tim Harris's phone rang at 22.10 hours. It was his friend in the Dutch Navy. "Good news, Tim. We have found your MTB265, just about where you said. A diver went down and took a photo of the number. I'll fax you all the details in the morning. It lies among rocks so I don't think it could be lifted."

"Thanks for doing that, it's important. I don't think we wish to raise her it will become a war grave." Harris took a beer from his fridge and sat for a while before retiring.

CHAPTER 8

Joanne arrived at her boat early next morning, calling to Carter as she climbed aboard. He poked his head out of the wheelhouse when told, "We are going to Cambridge today if you feel up to it."

Lt Carter asked if there was any news from Harris but Joanne said it was too soon and she would probably get a call later. Carter still wondered how her little mobile worked, thinking he must ask later. Once in the comfort of Joanne's BMW, Carter watched as she turned the key, put it in gear and away the car went. Carter then asked Joanne why she was not changing gear and when told it was automatic, he thought that was another marvel he had missed.

The lieutenant wondered exactly why a visit to Cambridge was necessary, and Joanne told him she wanted to gather leaflets and info about Lord Cummings work with the POW. He laughed inwardly, feeling that if he saw Cummings he would want to kill him but wouldn't know how.

Joanne found a parking space just around the corner from Cummings' office, and noticed the Jaguar outside. "I think Cummings is there," she said. At that moment her mobile rang, making her jump.

"Good morning Joanne, it's Tim Harris. I have some news for you — the Dutch Navy has found MTB265 right where you said. They sent me some photos to confirm it."

"That is good news. I'm out for the day but could I see you tomorrow morning."

Tim confirmed that and with a click he was gone. *A busy man*, Joanne thought.

"They have found your boat and have some photos," Joanne said to Carter.

Joanne, with Carter beside her, walked into Cummings' office, where a lady at reception asked if she could help.

"Well yes, I was wondering if you had any leaflets or prospectus about what you do. I've recently come into some money and thought some should go to good causes. I understand that Lord Cummings was some sort of war hero."

Carter did a little cough, which made Joanne grin.

"We do have a leaflet form with a donation section in it., Lord Cummings is in at the moment — would you like to see him? He could give you some advice."

* * *

Joanne and Carter entered a large ornate room where Lord Cummings sat.

"How may I help you?" Cummings said.

Carter could hardly hold back, but knew he could do nothing, as he expressed to Joanne quietly.

Joanne enquired about how someone would go about making a donation to the Ex POW Association, she waffled about coming into money and wanting to support a worthy cause.

"Money that is donated goes towards Ex POWs during hard times, plus other areas where we can help," he replied .

Carter stood close to Joanne, "Ask him when and where he was captured."

Joanne hesitated then posed the question. Lord Cummings told of being captured in 1943 near the French/German border while helping the Resistance. He didn't speak of Colditz.

Carter groaned at the Cummings' audacity, quietly wishing he could do something, anything, to force a showdown.

Joanne thanked Cummings and said that she would be seeing him soon for a proper formal meeting.

* * *

Outside Joanne and Carter made straight for her car. "It must have been very hard for you to have listened to him," Joanne said as they sat in the car. "I think we should get back as I want to phone Harris on what happened."

Carter was very quiet on the way back; Joanne realised he was thinking so she kept silent. Carter thought it was only four days ago that Cummings had betrayed his country.

They arrived at Joanne's house just before the rush hour. Carter marvelled at all the electrical goods, and when Joanne put 'Sink the Bismarck' on the TV, Carter sat animated. "Did this happen?" he asked Joanne, who replied it was an accurate account.

Joanne was preparing a jacket potato when the phone rang. It was Tim Harris saying he would like to come round at 1900 hours.

"That's fine. See you then." Turning to Carter who was just staring at the TV she said, "Harris is coming about seven o'clock," Carter looked up from the TV "let's hope he has some good news as well as some photos."

"You have been very quiet today," Joanne said.

"I've been thinking how I can get Cummings. I don't think I can do anything myself."

Joanne told Carter she was confident Tim Harris would do his best.

* * *

Promptly at 1900 hours the doorbell rang and Joanne greeted him. "Nice to see you. Come in, would you like some tea or coffee?"

"Nice to see you again," Carter said sarcastically to Joanne who ignored him.

Tim had obtained some pictures of MTB265, mainly for identification, showing how she was lying, with the anchor hatch missing.

"Would that be where my anchor pulled it off?" Joanne asked Harris. He thought it possibly was.

Carter, looking very closely over Joanne's shoulder, asked, "Were there any bodies?"

"Remember Carter, it was a long time ago."

"Yes, of course," Carter replied. "That part I can't get used to."

"I guess by that Lieutenant Carter is with us," Harris said.

"Yes, he's with us," said Joanne, sitting down at the table. "So what else have you got?"

Tim told Joanne all they had to date: Ann was checking some things at the British Legion, and Parker was going to

Brighton to see Lt Slater, who was the flotilla leader that night.

"Good old Slater, one of my best mates," Carter told Joanne, "He was at the briefing we always had before sailing; he would always give us last instructions."

Joanne told Harris what Carter had said, Harris wrote it in his note book. "I'll tell Parker before he leaves in the morning."

Joanne reported to Harris what they had done that day, and how it affected Carter, whom she thought would have killed him if he could.

"Tell Carter that if anything has to be done, this department will deal with it," said Harris writing more notes, "and be very careful. Remember a person cornered is twice as dangerous, and with that I'll take my leave and hopefully call you tomorrow evening." Harris left, leaving the photos behind.

"Well, what do you think?" she asked Carter.

"I suppose it's going fine, seeing as all these people don't know or have never seen me. I can only thank your father, and especially you for believing in me."

Joanne said it was too late to go back to the boat so Carter could stay.

"I am feeling tired now." He said, adding he was quite happy to rest on the settee.

Joanne agreed, and said she would see him in the morning.

CHAPTER 9

Lord Cummings entered his office wondering what all the fuss was.

"Good news sir," said the receptionist, "The admiralty rang, a Lt Parker, saying you might be interested to know the Dutch Navy has found MTB265, and seeing you were the last person to be on her, he would like to do a piece in the Navy news."

Cummings looked at the receptionist for quite a while, "Yes, good news," he said, and walked straight into his office, poured a whiskey and sat down, wondering how they came to find MTB265, then thinking of what had happened on the jetty at Salsause.

Maybe I should contact Lt Parker. I'll leave it until tomorrow, he thought.

Cummings looked at his diary, and seeing Joanne's name he thought it was strange to have the two things at once, but dismissed it, as they were entirely separate issues. It was normal for people to make donations.

* * *

Harris, Ann and Parker held their morning meeting,

writing any updates on the flip chart. "So what's the latest on Cummings?" asked Harris.

"I've contacted his office in Cambridge with the spill that MTB265 has been found and I would like to do an article about it as he was the last person on her," Parker answered.

"Good," said Harris. "Ann, have you anything?"

"Well yes, something we should check is how many agents might still be alive who served in Holland and Belgium. They might be able to help in some way."

"Good thinking Ann. Check the file list, if there are any try and see them."

"I have a meeting at the British Legion this morning, and then I'll check on the agents list," said Ann, gathering up her paper folder. "See you both later."

"Are you all set for Brighton?" asked Harris.

Parker picked up his folder. "Yes, I think I have all I need. Let's hope Lt Slater still has a good memory."

Harris decided to contact the Dutch security service, as Ann had enough to do. After a brief explanation about national security, Harris was told that the Dutch Government would help if possible, but he would have to go to Amsterdam as it was concerning Dutch citizens. He advised the Dutch authorities he would be arriving tomorrow and thanked them again for locating the MTB265.

* * *

Ann returned from the British Legion HQ, and told Harris that they would go through their records of POWs, and if he could give them a ring to verify all was in order, as they had to protect people's privacy.

"I have to go to Amsterdam tomorrow about their Resistance. They can only let me see what they have — can't do it by phone or fax. I can understand why."

Ann agreed she had plenty to get on with, checking any war-time agents who were still alive.

Harris said he would arrange with Parker for the Cambridgeshire police to keep an eye on Cummings, as part of National Security. He would call the Chief Constable on his return.

Ann returned to her office, sorting out what she had in the file of ex agents, enough to keep her busy for quite a while.

Harris gathered all the necessary paperwork he thought he might need, and after telling Ann he was going a little early to pack his bag and make a few notes, he headed for the local Chinese take-a-way, before going home.

While Harris was making notes, he thought he had better ring Joanne. He needed a little more detail to put before the Dutch Security.

Joanne was enjoying a cup of tea, while talking to Carter, when the phone rang.

"Hello Joanne, it's Tim Harris. I'm going to Amsterdam tomorrow and could do with a few more details on what happened. Could you ask Carter how the rest of the crew died?"

Carter explained to Joanne how Junior and the Cox'n were shot on the bridge by Cummings, the two ratings tending the ropes were shot by German troops running along the jetty, who also shot the forward gunner. Cummings, holding a pistol, told him it was "bad luck old chap, I've a good position waiting in Berlin." It all happened so quickly."

Joanne relayed this to Harris, who wrote it all down,

saying, "I have to have a good reason before the Dutch let me see any files on their wartime agents. I am hoping to find someone who may have known Cummings."

Joanne wished him luck as she said goodbye, then turned to Carter, "Well I think that's it for now. I thought we would go and see the sights of London tomorrow. The rest of today I'm going to relax." She put the TV on for Carter then made herself some dinner.

* * *

Joanne was up early the following day, and making sure Carter was all right, they set off for London. Carter was overcome with how things had changed, and kept stopping and looking in shop windows. He told Joanne he remembered Oxford Street with sand bags and shutters.

The day soon passed and Carter was getting tired, Joanne started for home, thinking she must try and get more time off work.

* * *

Parker arrived in Rottingdean on the outskirts of Brighton just after 11 am; he soon found the house he was looking for. He introduced himself as being from the Admiralty and asked if Mr Slater was available. His daughter, Emily Oswald, ushered him in, telling him to call her father Dennis, assuring him her father loved company and he was welcome to stay as long as he liked.

Brendan Parker greeted the old man with great respect and said he would like to ask him about his time on the flotilla that included the MTB265, mentioning that it had been recently found by the Dutch navy.

"Where did they find her?" asked Dennis.

"Among rocks just off Salsause," answered Parker

"That's where she was going." Dennis sat up, looking more aware.

"Can you tell me what happened that night?

"We had our usual briefing, and set off to wait for a German convoy which was going to Norway. Lt Carter was to go to Salsause as soon as the convoy was sighted to drop off an army major and then re-join me, but he never made it."

"Did you talk to Lt Carter about his Mission?"

"Yes, as flotilla leader I knew what he was doing — the CO insisted on that. I think it was something to do with centralising agents in Belgium and Holland for more control or something like that."

Brendan asked Dennis if he remembered Major Cummings and a list of agents that appeared to be kept at the time. Dennis recalled Lt Matthews of MTB285 once asked the Major how he knew all the names and places and he had said, "I have a list, old boy." Carter, his crew and the Major had not been seen again.

"Thank you very much for your time, I have all I want for now."

"Now Lt Parker, I may be getting old, but there's more to this then you're saying. We are talking about The Lord Cummings."

"Thank you again, yes there is more, but at this stage I can't say any more — but I will let you know the outcome. It may take a while, so bear with me."

Parker found a quiet spot among some rose gardens, and started writing everything down. Hearing voices he put the note pad away and started watching the croquet for 10 minutes before heading up the A23.

The office was quiet when Parker got back, other staff members from different departments were busy this way and that, Parker made himself a coffee and started putting his notes in order, when Ann came in the office with a bundle of papers. "Hello, I didn't expect you back so soon. Let me join you for coffee while you tell me all about the visit to Sussex".

CHAPTER 10

Lt Harris arrived in Amsterdam and was met by a man holding a board with 'Tim Harris' on it who said, "Hello, Mr Harris. I'm inspector Van Sause from the Security Service. Welcome to Holland."

"Hello," said Harris shaking hands. "Thank you for your time."

Harris was driven to an office building overlooking the harbour. He commented on the lovely view and the Inspector agreed and got straight to the point of asking how he could help Tim.

Harris told the story so far, without any names.

"Very interesting, if you find it true I think, my friend, you have a problem."

"Justice will be done if true, now everything at this stage is top secret, just in case it's proved wrong."

"Understood," said Inspector Van Sause.

The inspector then took Harris to a basement and into a long room full of boxes on shelves, leaving him with the archivist. Harris signed his name, adding the date and time and the files he would like to view. Tim requested files on the Dutch Resistance from 1942 to '44. The archivist made a phone call and told Harris not to remove files. He could make notes as long as he showed the Inspector before he left.

* * *

After about two hours Harris found only eight names of agents still living. He wrote down the names and last addresses, then went back upstairs and showed the notes to the Inspector, who asked his secretary to check and find out who lived nearby.

"While she is checking we can go to lunch. You can tell me more about your Lt Carter," said Inspector Van Sause. Lunch consisted of coffee and a Belgian bun.

"Lt Carter seems to be a ghost from 1942 who somehow broke loose from his sunken boat, due to Miss Kilmore's anchor, and through her comes the story."

The Inspector thought for a while, "She could not have made it all up, with agents and traitors, MTB numbers, locations, and naming this prominent person. How could she possibly know all that?"

"No, her story has too much knowledge of events not to have some merit," Harris answered. "I just want to get to the bottom of this. We are talking about a high profile person."

"Well, let's see if my secretary has come up with any local addresses."

His secretary was waiting. "Only three live in Amsterdam, one married an American and lives there, there is one in Reading, England, and the other three are scattered about Holland." Van Sause thanked her and informed her he would be out that afternoon but would have his mobile on.

* * *

Arriving at Hague nursing home, the nearest address, on the edge of a canal, they were shown into a reception area with a military theme about it.

A member of staff came and asked if she could help. After showing his police card and asking to see Mr Michael Voit. Harris and the inspector were shown into a bedroom where an old man sat in a chair next to a bed.

"This is Mr Voit. He's very frail, so please don't stay too long," said the staff nurse.

"Hello, Mr Voit, I'm Inspector Van Sause and this is Lt Harris from the British Admiralty. Could we ask you a few questions about your days with the resistance?"

"I'm a little forgetful these days, but will try to help you. So many years have passed."

"While you were with the underground, did you ever come across this man?" asked Harris showing an old photo of Cummings which he got from records.

Voit looked at the photo for quite a while. "Can't be sure — looks familiar. Thomas Burge is the man you want, he was our section leader."

VanSause looked on his list; Thomas Burge was not on his list of locals.

Voit again looked at the photo. "Was this man English?" he asked. "I seem to recall an English agent saying something about reporting, can't remember what. Thomas is the man who would know."

Voit looked very tired, the nurse came in and said he usually slept about this time and asked could the men leave and come back another day.

* * *

Outside VanSause asked if he could see the photo and

Harris showed him. "Can't say I recognise him anyway."
They both laughed.

Phoning Marguerite he asked for the address for Thomas
Burge."

"Are you still at the nursing home?" asked Marguerite.

"Yes, just leaving now."

"Good, just carry on along that road until you see a
church, turn right head towards the motorway, turn left at
the second junction, and go over the first roundabout to a
village called Lomover. Thomas Burge lives next to the
general store with his son."

"What would I do without you?" replied Van Sause.

Twenty minutes later they found the house they wanted,
tapped on the door. A young man answered, took them to
Thomas Burge who was tending his Roses. He invited
them to sit on a garden seat while formal introductions
were made.

"Your friend Mr Voit suggested we see you. He said you
were his section leader in the resistance."

"Yes that's right, quite a few years ago now," Burge said.
"I think it was because I was young and a school teacher."

Inspector Van Sause explained a little then showed Burge
the photo of Cummings.

Burge immediately smiled and told them it was a picture
of Hans Fletcher, sent over from England to do some
reconstructing. They had not got around to finishing it as
the Germans had a purge and most of the section were
captured or killed. He had escaped because he was seeing
a RAF pilot to a fishing boat that was waiting. That's when
he heard the news about the German roundup.

Burge suddenly became quiet.

"Do you know what happened to Hans Fletcher?" asked
Van Sause.

"He must have been killed or taken prisoner. I never saw him again. The underground was going through a bad patch at that time — English, Dutch and Belgian agents were being hunted. Times were very hard."

"Thank you, Mr Burge. If Lt Harris should ever ask you to go to England for any reason, would you be prepared to go?"

"Yes. My son would have to come, too. I'm fine for short periods, and then I get tired."

"Thank you again," said Harris.

* * *

On the way back to Amsterdam, Harris said, "Well that would all add up."

"Let's get back to my office and see if we can find any more underground teams that might have had the same problems," Van Sause answered.

"When we get back to your office I would like to phone my team, and see if they have any more information," Harris remarked.

Back in London, Ann answered the phone. "I've found three ex agents — two live near London, the other in Wales. Parker and I are going to see the two near London this evening."

"Well done," Harris replied. "I think I've had a good day here — found out quite a lot. See you both in the office tomorrow, good night."

CHAPTER 11

Joanne picked up Karen; it was a bright Saturday morning, a good day for some retail therapy and Karen asked if they were taking Carter. Joanne thought that a good idea and as they reached the boat she called out "Would you like to come shopping with us, or do you think it might be too much?"

Carter wanted to see every advance he could, he had missed so much being struck down at such a young age. He thought of his shipmates and was feeling humble by the time they reached the shopping mall. Carter looked around, stunned by the bright lights, colourful clothes, weird haircuts, rings in lips, everyone rushing in and out of shops.

"Times certainly have changed. The shops have lots of stock, and everyone has bags of goods," Carter mused.

"It's our turn now, so follow us," said Karen. "Maybe we could get you some new clothes." She and Joanne laughed.

"I don't think that would work," remarked Carter. "These will do just fine thank you."

They stopped at a café and the girls decided to have a cream cake with their coffee. Carter had not seen the luscious looking cake before and declared if he had a tummy it would be rumbling.

52

Joanne looked at Roger thoughtfully, "Carter, what was your sister like? I wonder if she is still alive," she asked quietly.

Carter sighed and said that he would like to know but feared it was impossible.

"Maybe tomorrow we could try and find out," Joanne answered.

They continued shopping, which took a long time, as Carter looked into every shop. "Amazing," became his only word.

After about four hours Joanne said they had better start for home as Carter was getting tired and beginning to fade. When they got home, Carter fell asleep and Karen asked where they could start looking for Carter's sister. They would have to ask more about his family when he awoke. Three hours later he woke and said his batteries were recharged, he certainly sounded brighter.

"Good," said Joanne. "I thought we could have a talk. Karen has gone to bed."

"Why not? You are taking me on trust after all." Carter sat on the chair opposite Joanne, and wondered what she would like to know. The next day Joanne and Karen would try to find out where his sister was, if she was alive. Another idea was to ask Tim Harris what had happened to Carter's agent father who left England before his last patrol.

Karen came into the lounge, "I heard voices. I overheard the last part — you never mention your mother", she said.

"My mother left Jersey just before war broke out. Ran away with a Frenchman — that's all I know, as war began my father, brother, sister, and the whole RNVR unit came to England."

"We will start with your sister. What was her full name?"

Joanne asked.

"Maria Carter, that's all. I don't know if she married a chap called Brian Arnold. She was seeing him the last time I saw her. He was in MGB's out on Dover."

"According to my father she did get married, probably to this Arnold. At least it's a start," said Joanne. "And maybe Lt Harris could find out what happened to your brother."

"His name is Richard Carter; he is two years younger than me."

Joanne put her laptop on the table and started looking for Maria Arnold.

Carter marvelled at what was happening. Suddenly a list of twelve Maria Arnold's came on the screen, some had middle names, but four were just Maria Arnold.

"Good," said Joanne. "Two have email addresses." She sent an email to both asking if they were born in Jersey and came to England early in 1940.

"That will do for tonight. Maybe tomorrow we will get a reply. Time for bed I think," Joanne said. "Tomorrow is going to be interesting."

CHAPTER 12

It was two days later before Cummings rang Lt Parker. "Lord Cummings here. I understand you have found MTB265."

"Yes," said Parker. "The Dutch Navy came across it on a routine exercise. I remembered you being on her when last seen, so thought you would like to know."

Lord Cummings was interested as to whether the MTB would be a war grave or whether she would be raised. He asked to be kept informed, his voice giving nothing away.

"Most certainly you will be the first to know," said Parker.

"I think he may have been fishing," Parker said to Ann. "He seemed worried we might salvage her."

"Well that will give him something to think about," replied Ann.

It was a busy day for the team, gathering all the bits and pieces and putting them in order, tying up the loose ends and a pattern was emerging that no POWs had ever heard of Cummings being interned with them, and a lot of agents had been imprisoned at that time.

"There's no record of any underground movement using Cummings' central control system, and if Cummings thought Germany was going to win he would not have bothered anyway," Ann replied.

"Just a thought," Parker said. "Would the Germans still have any records relating to agents or traitors?"

"Good thinking, Parker, I don't know. It's worth a try. They do have a library on war criminals — maybe something there."

Ann phoned the German security service, and asked for Inspector Ralph Lunds whom she had met at an anti-terrorist conference the year before, telling him a little of what they were investigating and could she send a Lt Parker over.

"Yes of course, I'll get someone to meet him. Just let me know what flight. Make sure he comes to Berlin."

Carter was getting restless at nothing happening, he confided to Joanne, who in turn to take his mind off the situation suggested they should try and track down Carter's brother.

Suddenly her laptop bleeped and Karen read the message.

"In answer to your enquiry, I came to England with my father and two brothers in 1940." Karen shouted that an email had arrived.

Joanne read out the email, saying that it looked promising and typing a reply that Richard Carter had been the brother of Roger and that he had apparently died in 1945.

Another email arrived, suggesting they meet at the Richmond Hotel in Portsmouth where Maria was visiting her grandson, a junior officer on a mine hunter, following the family tradition. Joanne arranged to be there the following evening and Maria began to turn back the years in her mind.

Roger Carter too went to bed and tossed and turned

H.P. Lawrence

wondering how Richard had met his end so near to the end of the war. His father, too - how had he died? So many questions, so many answers hanging on the words of Maria.

* * *

Parker, meanwhile, was ready for Berlin, his stay depending on the cooperation of his German colleagues.

"That's fine, safe journey, let's hope it is worthwhile," Harris remarked.

Ann drove Parker to Heathrow airport, inquiring if he had everything he needed.

"Yes. I'll give you a bell this evening, letting you know what I am doing. Any information relating to Agents in Belgium and Holland they let me see will be helpful"

"This has all been done before with the Germans, they were very helpful back then, so they might find something," said Ann.

Parker settled on the plane, making more notes of what he might ask. The flight was short, and Parker was soon going through security.

"Brendan Parker," said a voice from the side barrier.

Parker looked at a smartly dressed young lady in a grey suit. "Yes, that's me," he replied.

"Welcome to Berlin, I'm Freda Lomba," she said, holding out her hand.

"Hello. Thank you for meeting me," Parker replied.

"I have been assigned to stay with you while you are here, and to help you all I can."

Parker thought she really meant she would be observing him but just politely thanked her. Parker put his rucksack in the boot of Freda's car; they then made for the old registry and records office.

"There are still old records of the war years there that have not been seen since," explained Freda. "People are not interested any more. It's only when someone has a query like yourself — the younger generation just want to get on with living."

"Very wise," said Parker. "But something has cropped up that I'm hoping you can help me with, relating to a high profile person."

They went down some concrete stairs, along a passage with a big door at the end. "This is the old records store room, it's under the main building," explained Freda. She opened the door, switched on the light, and was looking at rows of shelves with boxes piled high on each. "I don't know where to start I've never been here before."

"Let's see if any boxes are marked with a date," Parker suggested.

After looking at a few boxes they found they all had dates, and some had names or places on them. "We are looking for anything between 1941 and 1944 regarding Belgian or Dutch agents killed or imprisoned, or someone named Cummings," said Parker.

It took the rest of the day without any luck.

"I think I had better stay another day, if that's all right with you Freda,"

"I thought one day was quick," she replied.

"Good. I'll book into a hotel if you can suggest one."

"No need, you can stay at my place," suggested Freda. "I share it with another police woman, she is on holiday so plenty of room."

* * *

Back at the flat Parker asked if he could treat Freda to a

meal.

"That's all right. I was going to make stir-fry tonight. Do you like it?"

"Yes, very much. I make it myself — it's easy for one," Parker answered.

"That's how I feel; will you have some red wine with it?" Freda asked.

"Lovely," Parker replied walking into the small kitchen. "Can I give you a hand?"

Over supper Freda asked Parker if the person he was investigating was well known.

"I can't say too much at this stage, but yes, he is well known," replied Parker.

"So it will probably be a big court case," Freda asked clearing the table.

"Possibly. It's too early to say — that's why we need any information from during those years. There are so many loose ends at present."

They settled down enjoying the wine and talking, Freda said she started in the Military Police, and then transferred to Homeland Security.

Parker explained he went in the navy straight from university, was second officer on a mine hunter, then first officer on a fisheries protection vessel, before moving to the Admiralty as a security officer, at present he was on loan to MI5, together with another naval officer who runs a department dealing with cold cases.

"Like the X Files you mean," asked Freda.

"Not quite, but maybe a little close," Parker answered.

"I've got a bed in the spare room, and the bathroom is next door."

"Thank you for making me welcome. If this does go to court we may ask you to come as a supporting witness," said Parker.

"That's fine, I'll give you my number, and you can call me anytime," Freda said, showing Parker his room, and giving him a goodnight kiss on his cheek.

* * *

Joanne and Karen, with Carter, booked a twin room for two nights at the Richmond Hotel in Portsmouth. After freshening up, Joanne went to reception and asked for Maria Arnold.

"I'll give her a call. I think she went to her room," said the receptionist.

"I'm nervous," said Carter, he stood beside Joanne as an elderly lady came towards reception. "It's Maria, only older."

"Maria Arnold?" asked Joanne. "I'm Joanne Kilmore. I'm sorry to bother you but I have some sad news on your family."

They all sat around a table in the hotel lounge. Carter sat next to Joanne but kept looking at Maria. Joanne ordered drinks, and began to tell Maria what had happened, but she didn't mention Lord Cummings.

"So how do I know this is true — it seems so absurd?" Maria asked.

Joanne turned to Carter and said softly, "Give me something about your time in Jersey."

"Ask her if she remembers mother leaving for France with Philippe Du'Rio on the fourteenth of March 1939."

Joanne asked Maria who began to weep a little. "I'm sorry," said Joanne. "That was a bit harsh. Would you feel better going to my room, it's a little more private?"

"Yes, that would be nice, I still find it very emotional."

Karen made tea as Joanne and Maria sat at the table. Asking Maria to believe that Roger was sitting beside her, Joanne held Maria's hand. She told her he wanted to see her again to know she was all right, and that he was very proud her grandson has joined the navy.

"Oh dear," said Maria. "It's all too much. What will happen to Roger?"

"We don't know. He gets very tired. He said he's fine, don't worry, and he is looking forward to seeing your grandson tomorrow. We will be looking from the side somewhere. I'll let you know what happens. Just remember Roger is fine," explained Joanne.

"The last time I saw Maria she was a pretty young lady, I'm glad I've seen her now and she is all right," Carter said to Joanne after Maria had gone. "I'm getting tired now, see you in the morning." And he turned in.

CHAPTER 13

Parker and Freda arrived at the library in Berlin, discussing how and what would be the best way forward, "I think anything to do with collaborators or traitors, there are so many boxes," Parker said as they started from where they left yesterday.

An hour later Freda pulled out a box marked 1940-1944. Lt Parker found the language difficult and asked Freda to scan through the box.

He continued looking in other boxes to no avail. Freda kept reading and writing notes all morning.

"I think it's lunch time," Freda yawned to Parker. "Do us good to have a break."

Over lunch Parker asked if he was staying the night, and could he buy a meal.

"Of course you are staying, stay for as long as you like," Freda said. "I did enjoy talking to you last night and look forward to talking more."

Back in the library Freda finally found another box marked in English, 1941 (code name Helper). Calling Parker they began to look through the documents. Freda started reading out aloud about an Englishman helping the German government.

"That sounds like what I'm looking for. Are there any photos or names?" Parker asked.

Freda looked but could only find a reference number 21447 and Parker asked if the document could be copied. A quick telephone call to her superior and she was told that anything related to "Helper "could be copied.

Finding a box labelled 21440-21490 they soon located the file and saw that an Englishman who helped capture agents in Belgium, Holland and France during 1941-43 was later given a position in Berlin with the German Intelligence, Propaganda Department. There he sat out the next two years, before going missing in 1945, believed to have returned to England. Parker felt a name must be mentioned somewhere.

After copying the file, they went back to Freda's flat to discuss what they had found, Freda ordered take-away meal, and settled down reading to whole file.

"This is a great help, at least we know someone was responsible for all those agents that were shot or captured," said Parker, pouring Freda another glass of wine. They read the same file over and over again, hoping to find something they had missed, but eventually gave up. They settled down on the settee, talking until finally falling asleep.

* * *

Joanne and Karen woke early. It was a lovely day — Portsmouth Harbour looked a picture of tranquillity. Carter was looking out of the window at the ships. "How they have changed," he said. "They are much sleeker."

"We could go and have a harbour tour after breakfast," Joanne answered as she made tea. "You would like that."

Carter was overwhelmed at all the shipping going in and out of Portsmouth. It made him so tired watching and he felt as though he was fading so they made their way back to the hotel before meeting Maria again.

Arriving at the hotel they saw Maria entering with a young Royal Navy Sub-Lieutenant.

"Hello," said Joanne, "this must be your grandson."

"Yes, this is Jamie. We have been looking over his ship. Jamie this is Joanne, the lady I was telling you about."

Carter whispered to Joanne, "This makes it all worthwhile. I'm very proud, but I must go for a rest now. Wake me before they go."

Joanne and Karen had a good talk to Maria and Jamie, who was very interested in his uncle Roger, "I would like some sort of potted history about him if you possibly could, something about his sea time."

"When all this is over I promise to give Maria the full story," Joanne answered. "At the moment it's very delicate."

Joanne and Karen went back to their room, where Carter was fast asleep. "Let him rest, we have another busy day tomorrow."

CHAPTER 14

"Good morning, Lord Cummings," the bank clerk said.

Wishing him a good day Cummings asked to see the manager, a Mr Fairfield.

Shaking Lord Cummings by the hand Fairfield ushered him into his inner sanctum and then asked, "Well, Ambrose, what can I do for you?"

Cummings said he wanted to invest in a foreign business and would like to transfer one million pounds into an account in Switzerland.

"That's a lot of money. May I ask what business?" the bank manager asked.

"Hotel and sporting complex in Germany near the Swiss border," Cummings said casually. "It's an all-weather complex."

"Sounds nice, it will take two days to finalise the transfer."

"That's good, I'll leave it with you," Cummings replied. "I have a busy few days ahead." Shaking Mr Fairfield's hand Cummings left, thinking that would set him up if he had to make a quick exit. He went straight home, packed a suitcase, put his passport and an address book in a small holdall, just in case... As he used to say to his friends, he would always be ready.

* * *

Parker arrived back at HQ to find Ann and Harris busy looking through files and asked what they were searching for.

"Trying to find more addresses of agents who are still alive," said Ann. "How did you get on in Berlin?"

"Very well. Freda is a lovely host," Parker said without thinking.

"Ann meant had you any information on our friend," Harris muttered, laughing. Parker told them the trip was very worthwhile and took the file from his briefcase. Everything they needed, but no name.

They all sat down and studied the file, finally Harris said, "I think we should try and get into Cummings' house, and see what we can find."

"Do you think after all those years he would have anything to incriminate himself?" Parker asked.

"What about his family? His wife died a while ago; he has two sons, both solicitors," Ann remarked.

Harris said they should be kept out of things for now and Ann said she would check to see if Lord Cummings had any appointments the following day.

Ann went to her office, Harris and Parker worked on a plan of action. "If all is okay we go tomorrow; if the house is empty we go in; if someone is at home we leave well alone. We don't want to draw attention to ourselves."

Harris decided to phone Inspector Van Sause, to ask if he could check with Thomas Burge to verify that he knew Cummings as Hans Fletcher.

Turning to Parker, "We now have two names for

Cummings, put them on the board so we can remember them. German records only mention someone called Helper — put that on the board too. What do we make of that lot? Parker how would you like another trip to Germany, or am I asking too much?"

"You must be joking, can I go now?" They laughed just as Ann came into the office.

"What's the joke?" she asked.

"Parker's off to Berlin again tomorrow," said an amused Harris.

"Well good news, Cummings is at a meeting all day tomorrow. Something to do with the British Legion, so if Parker's away I think we need another person," Ann remarked. "What I want you to look for is anything relating to Hans Fletcher. There's nothing in the files we have, so there must be more files. I'll let you make the arrangements."

Parker phoned Freda to ask if she would be free tomorrow, as he would be coming to Berlin. "I can be," she said. "It's quiet at the moment. Let me know what time and I'll meet you."

"Thank you. I'm looking forward to seeing you again," said Parker. Parker told Harris that Freda was going to meet him at the airport, and he would tell her what he was looking for then.

"What do you think, two inside Cummings' house, and one outside as lookout?" Harris said to Ann, who suggested young Robert Bourne from records. "He wants to get some field time in."

"Good idea. Get him up here and let's have a look." Robert was summoned. As it was roughly explained to him, Robert felt very privileged to be helping these men; he was on the way up the ladder now. He asked who should he seek permission from and Parker said he would see to all that. Robert had to be ready at 08.30, and would be briefed in the car on the way.

* * *

Joanne, meanwhile, was getting worried about Carter. He was getting more tired.

"Karen and I think we should get everything we have heard and done on a disc," she said, explaining to Carter what a disc was, as she started up her laptop.

Carter sat listening, saying he agreed, and would help all he could, "I'll tell you some personal details about my family, in case I'm not around long enough."

Roger Carter told them his father was the Commanding Officer of the RNVR in Jersey and himself and his brother Richard were junior officers. Once a year they travelled to Portsmouth for training on a large boat.

Joanne asked, "When exactly did your mother leave?"

Carter looked at the laptop screen. "I know it well. It was the fourteenth of March 1939, not long before war broke out. My father was very upset, and as war came he got very bitter, until he came to England and was then too busy."

"I'm sorry Roger, maybe we should keep to normal things," Joanne answered.

"It's all right, I don't mind, at least if you get all this down, someone might believe you, I would like to find out what happened to my father."

"Someone in the Admiralty is checking on that, a friend of Lt. Parker," Joanne assured Carter.

"Good, I really would like to know."

Joanne asked if there was anything else he could

remember, something amusing perhaps.

"We once had a slight mishap with the French navy in '38. We were on a training exercise in a converted trawler — a French destroyer told us to stop and boarded to check our boat. They thought we were a fishing trawler. I told them to stay clear as this was a Royal Navy training vessel and in the confusion I ran into their stern, damaging their rudder. Four days later the skipper of the destroyer came to Jersey and told my father that no action would be taken as it was a mix up on their part, much to the relief of the Jersey unit."

"Well if anyone doesn't believe me now, I don't know, it's not the sort of thing that is public knowledge," Joanne said.

Carter told Joanne about a young lady he used to talk to. "We would sit on the harbour wall in her lunch break, she worked in the NAFFI, she was about eighteen years old, name of Julie. I did arrange to see her again, but never made it."

"That's a shame. Sorry, anything else you can add?"

"My father had a tattoo on his left arm, tried to get rid of it. What a mess he made of it. It read, true love Yvette."

"I think that will do. How about a little tipple, Karen? I think we deserve one, sorry you can't join us Roger,"

They all sat down to watch TV, relaxing, another busy day tomorrow. Joanne wanted to find out about Carter's father.

CHAPTER 15

Lt. Harris, Ann and Robert Bourne arrived at Lord Cummings' house around 10.30. Ann had parked the car along the road out of sight of the house. "Now Robert, if you see anybody coming near the house use the radio quickly. If it is Lord Cummings, double quickly, okay?"

Harris went around the side of the house to the alarm box. *Good, government issue type*, he thought to himself as he deactivated it.

Ann had gone to the front door, rang the bell with no response, so she walked around the side looking for Harris, who had just finished sorting the alarm, "I think that should be all right, it's the same as the ones we train with."

They went to the back door; Harris had always found it easier to get in the back way,

Front doors were usually harder, once inside they could not hear any noise; Ann spoke quite loudly, "Hello, Police!" When there was no answer, she asked, "Where shall I start?"

"Start in the lounge. I'll start in this room, it looks like some sort of office room."

Ann walked into the lounge, and straight away called

70

Harris. "Come and see this."

Harris entered the lounge to see a suitcase and holdall on a chair, together with Cummings' passport.

They continued looking for anything that might be of interest. "I'll look in the bedroom" Harris muttered as he made his way upstairs, looking at the pictures on the stairway wall. "He's got some nice pictures here," he shouted to Ann, who had moved into the second lounge, which had a big china cabinet. In the drawers were tea towels, napkins and table cloths. In the bottom of one drawer was a box marked photos, she put the box on the floor and continued looking.

Harris came into the second lounge. "Not much luck upstairs. I think whatever we might be looking for is not here."

"Trouble is we don't know what we are looking for," remarked Ann.

"Okay, let's tidy things up here and try somewhere else," Harris said picking up the photo box, and opening it. "Might be a photo of Cummings in here."

They started looking at the photos. "Well, well, look what we have here," Harris said, showing Ann a photo.

Ann looked at it; it was a photo of Cummings and two German officers in uniform standing beside a staff car, all-smiling.

"Take the box, we can look through it properly later. Let's get out while it safe," Harris said, finishing and putting everything back as it was. Harris radioed Robert who answered that it was all clear outside.

Heading straight to Cummings' Office in Cambridge, Ann and Robert went in and asked the receptionist if they could make an appointment to see Lord Cummings.

"May I ask what about? Lord Cummings is a busy man."

"It's a little delicate, not too heavy though," Ann said looking at the desk diary that was open on the reception desk.

Fixing an appointment for the following Tuesday, a fifteen minute slot would suffice, Ann gave her name and left. Tim Harris presumed Cummings could not be leaving the country before then.

They headed back to HQ, looking at the photos on the way. There was three of Cummings with the two German officers. "I wonder who they are," remarked Harris.

"If we can't find anything positive by next Tuesday, I would suggest we cancel your appointment," he said to Ann.

* * *

Parker arrived at Berlin airport and was met by Freda who gave him a big hug. "What's kept you so long?" she said with a smile on her face.

"Lovely to see you, too," he answered getting into her car. "This time I am after anything relating to Hans Fletcher, as we believe he was known in Germany."

"First we go for lunch, on me of course," Freda answered as they turned into a hotel car park. "This is a good place. My mother used to come here with my father."

"Very nice, I'm glad you thought of this as it gives us a chance to talk," Parker said as he held her arm going into the restaurant.

They sat talking and enjoying a light lunch. "I suppose we had better get to work or my boss will wonder where I am," Freda finally said.

As they entered the library, Parker told Freda how much he had enjoyed lunch, and was looking forward to a quiet evening, just the two of them. Freda nodded, "me too."

It took three minutes before Parker found the box marked code name "Helper."

This could be interesting, he thought as he pulled out a file with the name Hans Fletcher. "Can I copy this" he asked Freda.

"Yes, I'm sure but I'll check with my boss," she said as she rang her superior. "That's fine, you can copy any file as before. It seems my boss has been told to help all he can."

Reading the file, it told of Hans Fletcher working for the Germans, under the name of "Helper." This is what he was after, but it didn't give any other name, they decided to read the whole file first before going any further.

While Parker was reading the file Freda continued looking.

"Come and look at this photo," he called to Freda. It was of two German officers standing beside a staff car. "I'll copy it as it was in the file. Let's call it a day. I've got plenty to read and digest for now."

"Good, maybe we can have a couple of hours before you go," Freda said.

"Or maybe I could get an early flight tomorrow," Parker replied leaning across the row of boxes and giving her a kiss.

"Maybe you could," she laughed. "I'll ring the airport and see what time there is a flight in the morning, now let's go and eat. Then we have the whole evening."

* * *

Next morning Parker was woken with a kiss and a breakfast tray. "Thought I'd treat you," Freda said.

"Thank you, Freda. I don't know when I'll see you again, not too long I hope. We have to get this case finalised."
Freda drove Parker to the airport. "I'll ring you this evening," he said, giving her a hug.

* * *

Arriving back at MI5 he was met by Ann. "Who's got a smile on his face then?" she said as they walked into the office.

"Any good news? We need some," asked Harris.

"Not sure, think so. Helper was also known as Hans Fletcher, no other name was found. He was working for the Germans, and this photo was in the file. It's of two German officers."

"It's them!" Harris exclaimed. "We have a photo of the two Germans standing with Cummings. Right get all this on the board, and see what we have so far." All they needed now was a sign that proved Cummings and Hans Fletcher were the same man.

As Ann was putting the latest information on the board, Harris asked Parker if he would ask his lady friend if she could find out if the two officers were still alive.

"I could always make another trip and find out," laughed Parker.

"First things first," Ann remarked with a smile, they all started laughing.

CHAPTER 16

Joanne, Karen and Carter arrived at the Admiralty at 10 am, "Joanne Kilmore to see Sub. Lieutenant Blunt please. I am expected,"

"Please take a seat. He will see you shortly," said the receptionist.

A young Sub. Lt walked in. "Hello, I'm Adie Blunt. Let's go to my office where we can talk. I understand you are interested in what happened to Lt. Commander Carter. Can I ask what is your interest, are you a family member"?

Carter leaned close to Joanne, "Tell him you are acting for his daughter Maria."

Joanne told Adie that his daughter and grandson, having got his first ship, were very keen to know.

After a few more questions Blunt asked them to follow him.

Once in Blunt's office, he pulled out a file. "This is the file we have on Lt. Commander Henry Carter; also known as Henri Cartier. Where would you like to start?"

"After he came to England, with his two sons and daughter," Joanne answered.

Blunt continued, "In 1942 Henry Carter was enlisted by Carisbrooke house, an intelligence establishment, where his talents as an artist were put to use. He was sent to Cherbourg in France where he already had a studio. He started painting German officers, with the harbour or other sea defences in the background, also what uniform they had, which told us what type of troops were there, he always painted a copy, gave the original to the German officer the other was put in a fisherman's marker buoy, which was picked up early Sunday mornings by one of our gunboats."

"So what happened to him" Joanne asked, "Did he return to England?

"Sadly no. In 1945, just before D-Day, he was arrested and shot."

Carter looked at Joanne, "Was it a firing squad?

"How was he killed? How did they find out he was working for the British?" asked Joanne, who wanted to know herself.

"He was seen in Cherbourg by a woman, known as Yvette Du'Rio, who we understand was in league with the Germans, along with her husband Philippe Du'Rio, who also was a French traitor."

"Mother," Carter whispered to Joanne. "No wonder he was bitter towards her."

"This Yvette, who turned him in to the Germans, did you know that she was Maria's mother?" Joanne asked.

"Yes, it's on the file, three children, Roger, Richard and Maria. The Germans raided his shop and found two of the latest paintings, also a marker buoy. He was taken away and shot by a firing squad. He provided a very valuable service. The British learnt quite a lot about what was happening in that part of France."

"Do you know what happened to Yvette?" asked Joanne.

"A little vague that bit. We believe she was killed by her

son Richard. He was sent over to Cherbourg to find out what had happened to Henry as we had not heard from him for a while, and we think when he got to the shop he found his mother and Philippe had taken it over. When Richard came back all he said was his mother and Philippe were dead,"

"Oh! And the other brother Roger was killed at Salsause while on a patrol," Blunt closed the file. "That's all we have, I hope it will do."

"Yes and thank you. I'll pass that on to Maria and thank you again."

Outside Carter was very quiet. "That was not what you expected was it?" Joanne asked.

"No." Carter answered.

"So what happened to Richard?" Karen asked.

"That, young lady, is something we have to find out," said Joanne. "Maybe I could ring Blunt and see if he can help. Now let's get home, I'll be glad to rest my feet."

Carter was still quiet, so Joanne thought she would leave it like that until they got home.

CHAPTER 17

Parker rang Freda. "Could you possibly find out if either of those German officers in the photo are still alive?"

Freda said she would try, but doubted if they were.

"Freda is checking, and will ring me as soon as she has something," Parker explained.

Harris was looking at the board. "That's good; we only need a name that could link Cummings to Hans Fletcher, or Helper."

Ann was looking over some papers. "It's funny no ex POWs heard, or saw Cummings in any camps."

"I agree, but we must make this case airtight," Harris answered.

Parkers mobile rang. "Hello Freda. Good news I hope."

Freda had found one gentleman still alive, living in Duisburg with his family. The other died during the war.

"One is still alive, living in Duisburg," Parker said.

Harris looked at Ann, and asked, "What do you think another trip to Germany?"

"I think it's time we sent young Robert," replied Ann.

"Not on your Nelly," Parker butted in. "I'll ring Freda. She will meet me at Frankfurt airport as soon as I get the flight time."

"Be careful with the German. We don't know how thick he was with Cummings," remarked Ann.

"Don't worry. I'll let Freda do all the talking."

"Just be tactful, don't get him on the defensive," Harris told Parker. "He could still be in touch with Cummings."

* * *

Parker met Freda at Frankfurt airport, and was welcomed with a hug. "His name is Stephen Hansel. He lives with his grandson who is handicapped with leaning difficulties, and his daughter-in-law lives three doors away. Her husband died six years ago."

"How will you ask the questions?" Parker asked.

"I thought I'd start by saying do you know that your friend died during the war, and see what happens from there."

Freda parked her car around the corner from the house. "Force of habit," she said to Parker. "I was trained never to leave your car outside the property you were going into."

Freda knocked on the door, which was opened by a big man about 35 years old. "Can I help you?" he said.

Freda showed her warrant card. "We would like to see Mr Stephen Hansel, please."

"Come in, he's in the garden. He's having a rest."

They followed the big man into the garden; Stephen Hansel was seated in an armchair under an arch covered with clematis.

"Hello, Mr Hansel, my name is Freda Lomba; I'm from the ministry of social affairs,"

Parker looked at Freda, nice one he thought.

"I'm looking into finding any relatives of this man." Freda showed Stephen the picture of himself with another

German officer and Cummings.

"Yes I remember him, Claus Schmitt, we were both working in propaganda media, I was his best man when he married. He was killed during the war."

"Who is the other man in the photo? He's not in uniform," asked Freda casually.

"That's an Englishman; he worked with us in propaganda, always saying he is getting some big position when Germany won the war."

"Well, thank you, Mr Hansel, we can work things out now, do you know the Englishman's name, just for our records?" Freda asked as they were leaving.

"Only knew him as Hans Fletcher, or Helper."

"That's fine, and thank you again," Freda said.

Elated, they left the house knowing at last they had the ID they wanted. The hotel which Freda had booked was select and intimate, over dinner Freda asked Parker who the person was and what he had done wrong.

Parker studied her face and gently said, "At the moment I can't tell you his name, only that he is a prominent person. If he is found guilty the British government has an embarrassing problem. I promise as soon as we are ready to I will let you know, as I expect you may be a witness of some kind."

"That's okay, I understand," said Freda. "Now let's finish dinner and have an early night."

* * *

Parker rose early the next day, showered and made coffee. "Good morning," he said to Freda, and apologised for waking her.

Freda turned over, "I'm awake. What time does your

flight leave? It takes about thirty minutes to get to the airport."

"The flight is due to leave at 1000 hours, we should get there at least forty-five minutes before,"

Freda drove slowly to the airport. "I'll miss you. Please give me a ring tonight."

"I don't know when I'll see you again. Let's hope we can get this settled quickly," Parker said as they arrived at the terminal.

Parker booked in, gave Freda a hug and said he would ring at 1900 hours.

Freda watched as the plane took off, and waved, before heading back to Berlin.

CHAPTER 18

"Ann," called Harris. "Glad you are in early. Could you contact the British legion HQ, and get some top man to come here? Say it's of grave importance. I think it's about time we filled them in, so get someone reliable we can trust."

"I know the very man, General Tasker. I met him at a conference and he was a POW in Singapore, a really nice man."

"Sounds just the one. Tell him it will be a confidential meeting."

"Parker rang last night, said he had some good news," Ann muttered to Harris as she looked for the Legion phone number.

General Tasker was not available so Ann left her extension number and asked for a call back.

* * *

Parker re-entered the office just as the phone rang.

"Hello Ann, General Tasker here. You wish to see me?"

Ann affirmed that he was needed at the office. "We have a matter of grave importance that we feel you should know about. Yes, 10.30 tomorrow will be fine. Look forward to seeing you again." Ann put the phone down. "Welcome back, Parker," she remarked with a little smile.

"Good morning, Parker. Let's see what you have," Harris said as they all sat at the table.

Parker began explaining that the two Germans in the photo were Lt. Stephen Hansel and Lt. Claus Schmitt, who both worked for the Propaganda ministry. The other man in the photo was known to them as Hans Fletcher, or Helper. Schmitt died during the war. This was told to Freda by Hansel. He still remembers."

Ann wrote on the board against Cummings' name, known as Hans Fletcher, also Helper, next to the photo, Hansel and Schmitt.

"I think it's about time I had a word with the PM," Harris remarked. "Ann, could you make some sort of file on what we have? I'm going to see Joanne Kilmore, to see if there is anything we have missed. Then please make an appointment to see the PM. Say it's very urgent, national security."

Ann took all the paperwork into her office and started making a copy file.

"Parker, would you mind the shop? Don't let anyone in except Robert Bourne. I've asked if he could be released to help us."

* * *

Harris arrived at Joanne's house just after lunch. "Hello again, sorry to trouble you."

After accepting a cup of tea Tim Harris told Joanne he was putting together a file to take to the PM and wondered if there was anything she could possibly add.

Carter was there and listening, he whispered to Joanne "I only knew Cummings for that one night, I met him in the NAFFI talking to some sailors, then we set sail and that was that."

Joanne told Harris, who wrote it down, "Maybe you have enough evidence already."

Harris answered, "We never have enough. What I'm going to do now is go and inform the PM with what we have, I shall be accompanied by General Tasker from the British Legion."

Joanne asked Harris if Cummings was found guilty what would happen to him due to his advancing years. His status and his family would all suffer too. The option besides jail might be that Cummings took the gentleman's way out.

"I suppose that would keep his family safe from the press?" Joanne said.

"Whatever occurs next, it's a bad business," Harris answered as he made his way to the door. "I'll make my leave, and will let you know what happens with the PM."

"Maybe I could find a way of killing Cummings myself," Carter said to Ann as they watched Harris leave.

"No way, that would make you as bad as Cummings. I'm sure Harris can take care of things," replied Joanne.

* * *

Arriving back at his office Harris found Parker and Robert looking at the board, still trying to conclude all the information pointed to Cummings. They decided there was no question, it did.

Robert was going to be sent to Cambridge to keep an eye on Cummings, needing now to know his every move. He might try to leave the country at any time. Robert was only too glad. *At last*, he thought, *a job on my own*.

"Ann and I will be seeing General Tasker tomorrow, and then we go and see the PM," Harris told Parker. "Could you check who the Solicitor for Cummings is? Let's cover all avenues — no last minute surprises."

Ann said that the PM could only see Harris at 1530 hours for ten minutes only.

"That will do for the first visit; it's just to fill him in on what we are doing, and what might happen in the next day or two."

"Right, thank you team. That will do for today, tomorrow we start again."

Back home Parker rang Freda and told her the net was closing in and she might be needed sooner rather than later, in London. They continued talking and Freda was very willing to cooperate, Parker hoped it was him she wanted to see, as well as help the case along.

CHAPTER 19

Robert Bourne arrived outside Cummings' office just as Cummings was getting into his car. He followed at a good distance, all the way to Stanstead airport. Robert quickly phoned Harris, and said, "He's going to Switzerland."

"Okay, Robert. Come back to the office. I'll get someone from our Embassy to see where he goes," Harris answered. He then rang the Embassy, explaining he was Lt. Roger Harris MI5 and he needed a security watch on a gentleman just leaving Stanstead, Flt No 0086. It was very important. He wished to know everywhere Cummings goes and who he will be seeing.

"That should be okay. Send me details and conformation," said the voice.

"This is national security, so be careful not to be seen, and thank you very much. Detail and a contact number is on its way to you now."

Ann was to be sent quickly to Switzerland on the next available flight. She was told to go straight to the Embassy and see what has transpired. If he had arrived Ann was to follow him, keeping Harris informed.

Robert arrived and took Ann to Heathrow airport, after which he went back to MI5 to look after the office while Harris was at his meeting with the PM.

General Tasker arrived for the scheduled meeting that afternoon. He greeted Tim and asked how he could help.

"I'm sorry to say it is disturbing," Harris said, laying the photos and file on the table. "A serious problem has come to our attention, which we believe is true. I would ask you to listen first and ask questions after, and I must tell you this is classified."

Harris told General Tasker what they had so far, including the photos. The General commented that this story had started with a young woman who fished up a ghost, and hoped he was sure of all his details as Lord Cummings was a prominent figure.

"We can tie Cummings to two aliases: one, Hans Fletcher, and two, Helper. The Admiralty has Cummings on file as an intelligence officer who persuaded them he should go to Holland and set up a new system for reporting, but most of the agents were shot or captured." Harris asked the General for any details of POW claims that Cummings had made and in turn he would tell the General of any further developments. Harris began to excuse himself, mentioning a visit to the PM and asked the General to accompany him.

* * *

They arrived at No.10 just before 3.30 pm. An aide said the PM would see them; he had a ten minute slot.

"Good afternoon, Prime Minister," said Harris, introducing General Tasker.

"Sit down both of you and tell me what's so important," the PM remarked.

After ten minutes the PM called his aide and told him to cancel his next appointment.

Two hours later Harris left No10, leaving a worried PM who had certainly listened with intrigue and concern.

Saying goodbye to General Tasker, Harris phoned his office and told Robert to lock up, apologised for the delay, and he would see him in the morning.

Harris made his way home to await news from Ann. It was nearly 2230 hours before she rang.

"Sorry it's so late but our boy has been busy. He's been in three banks making withdrawals. At the moment he's having dinner with two gentlemen. That's where I am now, sitting at the bar, and so far have had two propositions. Some sad people around." He could hear the laughter in her voice.

Harris rang off wondering why Cummings would want to get money out of the bank, and why did he have Swiss accounts? Ann rang again to quickly say the two strangers and Cummings had arranged a meeting at 10 am and she was on her way to the hotel, she would report back later the following morning. Parker entered the office and told them Cummings had his son Alex as a solicitor.

"I think another visit to his house tomorrow morning is on the cards," Harris said as Robert made coffee.

"Should we let his son know anything yet?" Parker asked.

"Not yet. I don't want to spoil his life unless I have to," answered Harris.

Ann phoned about 10 am, "Cummings and his two friends have just had breakfast, I've found out they are art dealers from Frankfurt."

"That's interesting. What would Cummings want with them?" Harris asked.

"I'm trying to find out their names. I've only heard them telling Cummings that they have just opened their sixth shop in Berlin."

"Well done. As soon as you get their names I'll ask Parker to contact Freda and see if she can find out anything about the art galleries." The rest of the day was spent getting Robert Bourne up to speed.

* * *

At 8.30 am the next day Harris and Robert arrived at Cummings' house.

"What are we looking for?" asked Robert.

"Anything you think might help any dealings with art galleries. Start upstairs and keep looking out the window in case someone comes. I'll start down here."

After about thirty minutes, Robert came down calling Harris, "got something here," he said, handing Harris a folder.

"Well, well," said Harris as he opened the folder, and looked at photos of paintings.

"Look on the back of the folder, something you might want to know," Robert remarked.

Harris turned the folder over and read the label, Gunter & Hass art dealers Frankfurt Germany. "I'll ring Ann. I'm sure those men are who Cummings is seeing."

Robert picked up a photo of three horsemen. He thought it was a picture of a famous painting he had seen on TV. Then he remembered, it had been on the television as he thought, in a documentary of Belgian art, believed stolen by the Germans years before.

"Let's get back to London. This is getting worse by the minute, and I'd better warn Ann to be careful just in case."

On the way back to London Harris rang Ann. "We think your two gentlemen are Gunter and Hass from Frankfurt, art dealers. We seem to have another problem. Be careful, I don't like the way this is going," Harris warned Ann.

Just as Harris and Robert were entering the car park at HQ, his phone rang. It was Ann, "You were right, the gentlemen are Hans Gunter and Heinz Mass. They are both art dealers from Frankfurt."

"Good. Stay with Cummings, and make a full report of everything he does. I'll get Parker to contact Freda, and see if she can check them out. Robert and I have some homework to do. Ring me if any problems."

Parker was waiting in the office with General Tasker. "Hello General," Harris greeted him.

"I popped in whilst passing. I could not find any real evidence that Cummings was in Colditz. I've spoken to a couple of men that were there, and they never saw or heard of him. They said they just thought he must have been as that's what he has always said."

"Thank you for your time and understanding in this matter. We will keep you informed all the way," Harris told General Tasker as he was leaving. He then asked Parker to phone the Dutch Embassy and ask if a senior official could come to his office and to then phone Freda to see if she or someone from her department could come to England. "Give them little details," he said. "It would make the German office more curious that way." Tim Harris was curious about Freda, as Parker appeared to be smitten.

Ann rang the office. "Cummings is getting the 1600 hours flight back to Stanstead, and I've managed to get on the same flight. No4367."

"Robert, you pick up Ann; Parker, take another car and follow Cummings. If he goes home then you come back here. Sorry for the late night."

"What if Freda rings?" asked Parker.

"I'm sure I can handle it — maybe find out what she thinks of you," Harris laughed, just as the phone rang.

Things were really stepping up a gear now with a message that the Ambassador himself was arriving from the Dutch embassy and another from Freda's department saying they would consult Berlin and get back to him.

"Thank you very much for your assistance, very kind of you," Harris put down the phone. "Tea time, I think, while we wait."

They sat looking at the board. "What next?" said Harris.

CHAPTER 20

Carter was getting tired more often; he said to Joanne he hoped to last long enough to see justice done.

They sat talking about how things have changed since Carter's days.

"When this is all over, if I last that long, take me back to my boat, that's where I belong, with my crew."

"I'll take you back, and I'll ask Lieutenant Harris to come along as a good gesture, seeing he did believe us," Joanne assured Carter.

"That would be nice. MTB265 is a war grave now, so it's only fitting I should return."

* * *

Freda phoned at that moment. "Good evening Lieutenant Harris, this is Freda Lomba, I've had a word with my superior and he suggested that he would come over with me as it is a delicate matter."

"That's fine, I'll get Parker to pick you up. Just let him know what flight. I'm sure he is longing to see you," replied Harris. Being told the booking had already been made, Freda was assured that flight number 8734 would be met.

92

Ann arrived back, Parker rang saying Cummings had gone straight home, so was also heading home, and would see them tomorrow.

"Some good news, Freda is coming over with her boss tomorrow. You can go direct to Heathrow, flight number 8734, due in 0930 hours, that's if you want to," Harris said.

* * *

Next morning they all arrived early. Ann copied the file so Freda and her boss had one, Harris and Robert decided that a bigger table was wanted, so raided the office down the hall, together with some better chairs.

With the new table in position, Ann moved the flip chart board so they could all see.

"Put a cover over it until it's needed," remarked Harris.

"I'll get coffee ready and organise some lunch," Ann suggested. "It could be a long a day."

* * *

"Good morning, Freda," Parker said giving her a peck on the cheek.

"Good morning, Brendan, this is my director, Captain Houyt," she answered with a little blush. "Nice to see you again."

"Good morning sir, pleased to meet you," Parker said, shaking his hand.

"And you, I've heard a lot about you from Freda, and yes, all good."

Harris greeted them and introduced Ann and Robert. "Nice of you to come, I thought it's about time to put you in the picture. We have been asking a lot from your

93

records, so down to business."

Harris started from the beginning, with the occasional break to answer questions.

"So," asked Captain Houyt, "do we meet this ghost of yours?"

"You can't see him. That pleasure only goes to Joanne Kilmore and her niece Karen. I realise it's hard to understand, but it was Miss Kilmore who came to us with the story, and on checking, things have fallen into place."

"Sorry to interrupt; it was just a thought," remarked Houyt.

Harris continued, "I will now reveal our suspect. In front of you is a folder with photos and documents. Our suspect is Lord Cummings, director of ex POWs and a high profile person, so this is a very complex case."

Captain Houyt looked at the photos. "So these two German officers along with Lord Cummings worked for the Propaganda Ministry. I understand you took a statement from one?"

"Yes, it's in the file," Harris said, "next to last page."

There was a knock on the door, and a note was passed to Harris. "Ann, can you take over? The Dutch Ambassador has just arrived, I'll catch up with you all shortly."

"Sorry I'm late, had an important phone call from my ministry," the Dutch Ambassador said, greeting Harris with a firm handshake.

"Thank you for coming," Harris said showing him to another room. "I have some photos for you to see, and wondered if they have any interest to you."

The Ambassador looked at the photos. "Where did you get these?" he asked. "They are of Dutch Masters which were stolen during the German occupation."

Harris explained that with the help of the German

security service they are following some leads.

"This has been a headache for the Dutch, trying to locate items stolen during those times, please keep me informed."

"I will, and thank you for your time, you will be informed as soon as we are," Harris answered.

Back at the meeting, Tim Harris related, "That was the Dutch ambassador, which brings us to the next item on the file. During our search of Lord Cummings' house we came across some photos, copies of which you have in the folder, of Dutch masters, stolen during the occupation. Ann followed Lord Cummings to Switzerland where he withdrew large sums of money from different banks and stayed at a hotel with two German art dealers, Gunter and Hass of Frankfurt."

"Interesting," said Captain Houyt. "Freda, a job for you, look into the dealings of Gunter and Hass. I agree we should work together on this, we on the German side, will of course keep you informed. I'm sure Freda could do that," he went on, looking at Parker, "and now to bed. I'm booked in at the Langham, only me, I think Freda has made her own arrangements."

Parker looked at Ann and Harris and smiled.

CHAPTER 21

Next morning Parker said goodbye to Freda and Captain Houyt, as Harris had another appointment with the Prime Minister.

"So Lieutenant Harris, have you got enough to arrest Lord Cummings?" the PM asked.

"I'm positive. I can arrest him on receiving stolen goods, namely Dutch art, and once back at MI5 turn it around to being a traitor to the crown, and see what happens," Harris answered.

"Run through what you have in mind, just so if any questions are asked I have the general idea."

"We will go to his house and arrest him under receiving stolen goods that will give us at least forty-eight hours to bring in other charges."

"What if he calls his son? He's a legal chap."

"I've been thinking about that. I'm undecided, do I inform his sons or wait?"

"It could get nasty and embarrassing for the government if it goes to court," the PM replied.

"I'm hoping it won't go that far, I intend to offer him the gentleman's way out, if you agree, sir."

The PM thought for a moment, "Things like that I will

leave to your department, but we should protect his family."

"At all costs, I agree," Harris said. "We will be very discreet, and thank you, Prime Minister. We will keep you informed all the way."

* * *

Back at MI5 Harris started explaining the next move. "Okay, this is the plan: Ann and Parker will come with me to arrest Cummings; Robert, I want you to get an interview room ready. We will pick him up before he goes to his office."

"What if there are other people at his house?" Ann asked.

"Let's wait and see," answered Harris. "We must remember he can ring his solicitor, namely his son, so we must handle it delicately."

"Morning coffee and time for a little break while we reflect on what we have?" suggested Ann.

"Ann, before that could you ring Joanne Kilmore and ask if she could be in my office by midday tomorrow, and to bring Carter? The PM is worried as Cummings is an elderly man and maybe too frail to stand trial."

"It probably won't come to trial, because of the public humiliation for his family."

It was decided that the office Cummings used in Cambridge would be closed down immediately; telling the police force there it was a matter of security at the highest level.

* * *

At 0800 hours the next morning, two cars left MI5 heading towards Cambridge. One had Harris and Parker, the other Ann and Robert, who would bring Cummings back.

They were just entering Cambridge when Parker's phone rang. It was Freda and she was trying to get a message to Tim Harris. A raid had been carried out at Gunter and Hass, the art shop in Frankfurt. A basement full of paintings, statues and other art treasures had been found along with a ledger of sales with Hans Fletcher's name as a partner. Both men were now in custody. Freda suggested it should be left another day before Cummings was arrested, after questioning Gunter and Hass might throw more wood on the fire.

"Nice going, Freda, what next? I'll leave Cummings for another day," replied Harris.

"We are getting an expert to look at all the items, including the Dutch and Belgian authorities. If proved to be war trophies we will hand them back. I want to ask Gunter and Hass what involvement Hans Fletcher has in the shop. I'll ring again about midday tomorrow. Could I speak to Parker now, please?"

Harris handed back the phone. "Right lets head back to HQ."

"Hello Freda, are you all right?" Parker asked.

"Yes, I'm fine, we have just taken Gunter and Hass into custody and closed the shop while our experts examine everything there. I'll ring you later tonight."

Harris phoned the car behind. "Going back to HQ, will try again tomorrow, awaiting more info from Freda. I'll ring Joanne and tell her to leave it another day."

* * *

Carter told Joanne he was glad to leave it another day. "I'm getting very tired, and a good rest might charge my batteries."

Joanne explained to Carter, "I must contact work and say I won't be there for another week. I'm lucky, my partner Julie can look after things as it's quiet at the moment. We run a training school for young seamen."

* * *

Back at HQ, Harris was getting a little worried. Tomorrow was Friday and what if Cummings goes away for the weekend? "He does have a cottage in Devon, more like a small farmhouse."

"That might be worth a look sometime," Parker answered.

"I think he has an elderly couple minding it, but yes I think we should one day have a look," replied Harris.

That evening Freda phoned Parker, "I'll be over tomorrow, at Heathrow at 1100 hours, I've got a folder that you will find interesting."

Parker and Freda talked for two hours, before Freda said goodnight and she would see him tomorrow.

CHAPTER 22

The next morning was busy in the office. Harris and Ann moved the table and chairs so they could all see the board with photos and arrows pointing in all directions.

Harris was enjoying a coffee when his phone rang.

Parker said he would notify him when he was nearly back at the office. When he arrived at Heathrow he heard Freda's flight had landed. He saw her and waved, and she started walking faster until she cleared the barrier and into Parker's arms.

"Lovely to see you," said Parker.

"Lovely to see you. I've missed you," she answered.

"Everything is ready to get moving now; we were going to arrest Cummings yesterday until you rang."

"I think it was worth it, I have some news and some requests, my superiors have written a letter to Lieutenant Harris, so enough of that till we get to HQ, let's talk about us."

* * *

"Right," said Harris to Ann, "They are on their way, let's get the tea and biscuits ready, and I want Robert to come in on this. It's about time he had a proper job. Let's see if we can get him transferred to our department."

Ann left leaving Harris to wonder what Freda had that was important, was it an excuse to see Parker, or both.

"Hello Freda, nice to see you again," Harris said as they came into the office. "This is young Robert Bourne, he will be working for this department from now on. Ann is just making coffee, and then we can start."

Freda put photographs and a pile of paperwork on the table. "As you know we raided Gunter and Hass art gallery, mainly looking for any Dutch paintings that may have been stolen. Well, we found more than we expected. This is a copy of the ledger which contains names of paintings, the artist, sold to, how much, all going back to 1950, aswell as and who bought them. The money was shared between Gunter, Hass and Hans Fletcher, paid into a Swiss bank."

Everybody was silent for a moment, and then Harris spoke.

"Well, quite a surprise. What's your next move?" he asked.

"We have experts looking at all the ceramic art, to see if we can find out who they belong to. All paintings and other art that has been sold we will follow through. As regard to Lord Cummings, my superiors have suggested that if you find it a little difficult to prosecute him, we could do it under Hans Fletcher."

Another silence, Harris walked to the board. "A nice one, but we intend to charge him with being a traitor, and art theft. We could always say that the German government wish to question him about Dutch and Belgian war time stolen art, selling for profit, we have to be careful as he is eighty-eight years old, a little frail. A prison sentence would not be very long. I would suggest to him to help protect his family he took the gentleman's way out."

Freda picked up an envelope. "My superiors said I could stay here until the outcome. If things don't work out in your favour this is an arrest order for Lord Cummings, to answer charges relating to war time stolen art. We are sure it will not come to that, so I'll keep it in my bag."

"I think that's it for now," said Tim. "Meet here 0800 hours tomorrow, with two cars. Let's go and pick up Cummings. Ann, ring Joanne and ask if she can come in Monday about midday. Freda, I assume you have somewhere to stay?"

"Yes, with Brendan," she smiled. "It cuts cost."

They all laughed as the meeting ended.

* * *

Parker wondered where would she like to go and eat but Freda loved curry as he had found out, so they settled for yet another take-away meal. Brendan would later wonder if Freda ever did cook.

"Good evening, Mr Parker," the gent behind the counter said, "and is this young lady — the one you have been bragging about to my wife?"

"Yes Jimbo, this is Freda." They shook hands and Jimbo told them that this meal was a treat from him, as he wished them good luck.

Parker and Freda sat eating their Indian meal and a glass of wine, enjoying each other's company.

"What do you think will happen to us when this is all over?" asked Freda.

"I've been thinking about it too, with me here and you in Germany, both with the same sort of jobs. Only I'm still in

the Navy, just attached to MI5. Harris and I deal with
unusual cases such as this one. Harris has a sense for
strange things, so maybe I could get another posting."

"That would not be fair, you could stay with Harris, and
I would willingly give up my job to be with you."

"Things will work out; let's have another drink and enjoy
seeing if we have a future together."

CHAPTER 23

Everything was ready by 0730 hours; Harris had left word with the PM's secretary as to what was happening.

The two cars set off for Cambridge. Harris checked his pocket, "Don't want to forget the arrest warrant — got to be accurate with people in his position."

At 1000 hours they pulled up outside Lord Cummings' house. "A lot of cars here," Harris muttered, knocking on the door.

"Could I see Lord Cummings please?," asked Harris?

"I'm afraid he's not well, the doctor is with him now. I'm his son Matthew, can I help?"

Harris showed his warrant card, then said to Ann, "Have a word with the doctor, ask his condition."

Mathew Cummings remonstrated that he was not only his son but his legal representative.

Harris looked at Parker, before answering Matthew, "Check on Ann. Freda, you stay with me while I explain to Matthew Cummings."

Matthew took Harris and Freda into the study, which Harris recognised. "Now what is the problem?" he asked.

"Depending on how ill your father is," Harris began, "we have come here today to arrest him on suspicion of

104

receiving and handling stolen goods."

"My father's an old man and has no need to handle stolen goods; he is wealthy in his own right."

"Quite," Harris said. "But I wonder how he became wealthy?"

"I must protest as his solicitor, that he says nothing until I have spoken to him."

Ann appeared. "The doctor has called for an ambulance, and he's going to hospital, suspected angina."

Harris asked Matthew Cummings if he could come to his office on Monday about 11 am. "I understand you have a brother, it would be better if you could both come."

"Depending on how my father is," Matthew answered.

Harris suggested to Parker they go to see the Chief Constable, and try to obtain a 24-hour watch on Cummings.

* * *

The CC sat at his desk staring at the Warrant card and arrest warrant. He was concerned at the cost of such protection but Harris assured him that it would be met by MI5. Harris told the CC about the stolen art treasures and the need to make sure that Lord Cummings remained in England. They both agreed that Lord Cummings was a much respected man and the need for confidentiality was of great importance until they were 100% sure that the facts were established. On the way out Harris asked if they would let him know if there was any change in Cummings' medical condition.

"At least we have somewhere to go," Parker said as they sped off towards HQ.

Freda and Parker decided to see a west end show. Freda

said she had never seen one. After phoning around they managed to get tickets to see Cats. Parker said they should go and have a meal first, making an evening of it.

* * *

Harris contacted Derek Kilmore, saying he would like to see him again and was greeted warmly the next day. He apologized for intruding and said he would like to look at the photos of MTN265 and her crew. Derek had already contacted Joanne who had said she would call with those she has.

Joanne arrived about an hour later. "Hello Tim, nice to see you again."

"Nice to see you too," Harris answered.

"I've brought the photos. What's the latest?"

"Lord Cummings is in hospital with suspected angina. There is a twenty-four hour watch on him. I will be told if any change, and how's your friend Lieutenant Carter?"

"He's getting weaker quite often, and wants to get back to his boat with the rest of his crew."

"We are almost there. This little hiccup with Cummings put us back a couple of days'"

"You are staying for dinner," Derek asked. "Joanne has bought some nice steak."

"Sounds good to me. Can I get a bottle of wine from somewhere?"

"Don't worry about that, Joanne bought some back from Holland, so I have plenty."

"Well just a little one for me as I'm driving," Harris said.

"You could always stay here the night, plenty of room. You stay too, Joanne, someone to talk to," Derek answered.

Harris looked at Joanne and grinned. "In that case, open

106

the bottle. Matthew Cummings is seeing me at HQ on Monday morning. He is also his father's solicitor. I am going to tell him about his father, and see what happens."

Derek listened to Joanne and Harris over dinner, and thought it was about time she took interest in someone again after the last one, a city financier who thought the world revolved around him.

"I think the only way is to tell his sons the truth. They are well educated, so should understand your position," Derek muttered as he began clearing the table.

"I would like to tone it down a bit, but the German side is now involved."

"What will you do if Cummings doesn't pull through this angina?" asked Joanne.

"I've discussed this with my team and the German side; they are going ahead with their side of things, and find out what part Cummings played."

"Very complicated," Derek said.

"You're right, his sons should know how he became rich, and how he tricked the British people for so long. I just hope he lasts till I can interview him," Harris remarked.

"I'll leave you two for now, get back to my game of chess with Vincent. He always beats me, but we enjoy it. See you in the morning, good night."

"Dad plays on line with Vincent. He only lives next door — they sometimes go on for days," explained Joanne.

The next morning Joanne cooked breakfast. Tim Harris said how well he had slept and what a change it made to finally unwind.

As he was leaving he told Joanne he would ring Monday after he had seen the sons.

"Give my regards to Lieutenant Carter, and thank you again for a lovely evening."

Joanne gave Harris a kiss, and thanked him for believing in Carter.

CHAPTER 24

Parker and Freda were first into the office on Monday morning. "Everyone's late this morning," he said.

"It's probably done them all good to have some spare time," Freda replied.

"Morning people," Harris came strolling into the office. "Nice one."

"Sounds like you had a good weekend," remarked Parker.

"A very good weekend, it has done me the world of good, thank you."

"Probably a woman involved," said Freda.

Ann came in at that moment. "What's so funny? Have I missed something?"

"Not at all. Tim said he had a very, very good time at Chatham," replied Parker.

Parker said they should get down to business; they expected Matthew Cummings that morning and thought the other brother Andrew might attend, too. Ann told security who to expect. Freda began her list of questions, too.

Harris suggested they sit round the table as before. He would begin by telling of when Lord Cummings was

Major Cummings getting aboard the MTB265, then go through the agents that were killed or imprisoned, right up to the stolen paintings. Freda could then tell of her involvement, the ledger and a few photos could be shown and they would watch the reactions.

Ann made morning coffee with the help of Robert, who was late.

"I'll sit them opposite myself and Freda. Robert can get some good practice, sit at the end and take notes of all you hear, but not my opening spiel."

Coffee over, Harris and Ann sorted out paperwork. "I think that will do, everyone have five minutes to relax."

The phone rang. "Thank you. Ann will be right down to sign them in. The sons are here."

"Good Morning, Mr Cummings," Harris said, shaking Matthews's hand. "And this is your brother, Andrew?"

"Yes," Andrew said. "What's this all about? We have to see our father later."

Harris pointed to the chairs, and introduced Freda Lomba, Brendan Parker, Ann Johnson, Robert Bourne and then stated his involvement.

Matthew Cummings sat taking notes; Andrew sat listening more intently.

Harris picked up a photo of two German officers with Cummings.

"Do you recognise anyone in the photo?" he said showing first one then the other.

"Yes, that's our father. I don't know who the other gentlemen are," Matthew remarked.

"Those other gentlemen are German officers who worked for the Propaganda Ministry during the war years," answered Harris.

"What are you saying?" Matthew said, looking Harris

straight in the eye.

"I am saying that we have proof that your father was a traitor to the crown, from 1941 through 1945, working for the German Propaganda Ministry along with these two German officers. They also stole national art from the occupied countries. Your father was never in a POW camp. This he made up in 1945 when the war was nearing its end. He came back to England claiming to have escaped from Colditz."

"Show me the proof!" Matthew shouted.

It took another two hours of reading files and looking at photos before Matthew turned to his brother, "You've been very quiet. Don't you have anything to say?"

Andrew looked around the table, "I'm glad it's in the open now. Between you, me and father, I've known for many years that father was a German agent, and about his dealings with Gunter and Hass. When I was fourteen father took me to Frankfurt and I met them. They talked about selling more paintings. They were having wine and talking freely, I think forgetting I was there. I overheard him saying that if only Germany had won he would be in a very high position, but couldn't grumble as the paintings and art keeps him very wealthy."

"Why didn't you tell me?" Matthew asked.

"Because I turned off, didn't want to know, that's why I moved away."

"So what do you intend to do?" Matthew asked.

"Depending how your father is, we will talk to him, then decide."

"Will I be able to represent him?

"Only as his solicitor, not as his son. Freda, is there anything you wish to say?"

Freda looked at the two sons. "Whatever happens here I

will be asking your father about his friendship with Gunter and Hass. There are serious crimes that your father has been involved in."

The phone rang. "Excuse me," Harris said. "Yes, fine, we will be there about four pm." He hung up. "Lord Cummings has left hospital and on his way home. He can't understand why he has a police presence. Parker, organise transport, two cars as before."

He turned to Matthew and Andrew. "I expect you wish to get away, we can finish this later."

Matthew and Andrew left. "If my father is not too good I will object to you talking to him," Matthew said as a parting word.

* * *

Just after 4 pm they arrived at Lord Cummings' house, to find the Chief Constable outside, stating as chief constable of the county he would like to be there at the arrest.

Matthew and Andrew turned up just as Harris was entering the house. "Blast" he said.

Inside Lord Cummings was sitting in an armchair. "How are you father? Matthew asked.

"Not too good, they said I need a heart bypass, but will discuss it because of my age. Who are all these people?

Harris stepped forward. "Good afternoon, Lord Cummings. My name is Lieutenant Tim Harris, Royal Navy, attached to MI5, and I have come to arrest you on suspicion of war crimes, and dealing in stolen art from Holland and Belgium."

Harris read out the charges including the killing of the crew of MTB265.

"I see. You have proof, of course?"

"We have proof," Harris answered.

"And what is this art thing?" Cummings muttered.

"I'll let Freda Lomba from the German Security Service explain that," Harris answered.

Freda explained that Gunter and Hass were in custody, the shop in Frankfurt had been searched and paintings and other art are being studied by experts, as well as a ledger with names, dates, prices and sales, also other names involved, who will be arrested as soon as Freda got back to Germany

"Matthew, is there nothing you can do?" Cummings asked his son after sitting looking as though he were miles away.

"Are you saying it's all true?" Matthew replied.

Cummings looked at his two sons. "Germany should have won the war. I wanted to be on the winning side, and the stolen art kept us all in a wealthy life style."

Matthew looked at Andrew, and then to his father. "I'm afraid I can't help you anymore."

Matthew put his arm on his father's shoulder. "Andrew knew this since he was fourteen, but I had no idea."

"Pass my tablets please, for the heart."

Harris thought, *should I let him take his tablets… yes, the gentleman's way out.*

Cummings died 20 minutes later from a heart attack.

"Not quite the ending we were expecting" Harris said. "We will try and keep things quiet as much as possible. There will not be a high profile funeral, just your family. I have to inform the PM, the British legion and a few others." Turning to Matthew he continued, "Come and see me sometime next week, we can finish what we started, and get this finalised."

The chief constable said he would wait for the coroner,

and asked that Harris send him a report at the conclusion.

"Robert, your big moment, would you go and search Cummings' office? Look for anything to do with the case, maybe diaries et cetera, and then report back to HQ tomorrow."

"Parker, I'm sure Freda could do with your company in Germany, while she sorts that side out. As for me I'm going to see the PM and then I have a duty to perform for Lieutenant Carter, deceased."

* * *

The following morning Harris took his report to the PM.

The Prime Minister said it was probably the best outcome, as it could have been embarrassing for the government and the British legion. He thanked Harris for the way it was handled. "Just glad no other people were involved," he said as Harris said goodbye.

CHAPTER 25

Joanne was surprised when Harris rang and said he would be at her father's house about 6 pm that evening.

"Joanne has cooked a lamb stew, just for you," Derek Kilmore said greeting Harris.

Harris shook his hand and greeted Joanne, giving her a peck on the cheek.

After dinner Harris explained what had happened. "I don't know how Carter will take it. Parker and Freda are clearing up the German side, the PM's happy, so hopefully tomorrow we can help Carter get his peace."

They stayed up late sorting out tides and weather. "Looks like it should be okay," Derek said. "I'm off to bed; see you in the morning."

Joanne and Harris stayed up a little later, talking about how things had happened.

* * *

The next morning was bright with a very light wind expected. Derek would like to have gone with them but Joanne thought Karen would be there.

When they arrived at Joanne's boat young Karen was

waiting with Carter, very tearful as she would miss this kind man who she learned to look for and listen to, when others couldn't. It had made her feel special and she would remember all her life that there are some things that cannot be explained.

Harris told of all that had happened, and hoped some justice had been done.

Carter told Joanne, it was not what he expected, but he was glad it was finished, he could rest now.

The journey to Salsause took quite a while. "Getting close," Joanne said checking the charts. "I'm sure this is it."

"This is the spot," Carter answered, and sadly he uttered his last words. "Thank you Joanne and Karen for all your help, and thanks to Lieutenant Harris for believing in me. GOODBYE."

There was a silence as Carter returned to MTB265, to join his crew.

Joanne cuddled into Harris's arms. "Goodbye, dear friend." Karen sat crying as she threw a white rose into the sea.

Harris gave a salute. "Let's go home, it's been enough for us all."

Back at Chatham Joanne asked Harris, "Stay with me tonight, I feel very sad; I've lost a close friend."

* * *

Freda decided to pass all her information regarding the art case to her superior Captain Houyt, who understood. She left her department and came to England with Parker, and joined MI5 as an adviser and training officer in Harris's department.

Ann carried on as usual; Robert got promotion after his

good work in tidying up loose ends, and is now a member of the team.

Lt. Roger Carter is finally at peace.

* * *

Later the phone rang. "Is that Harris's department?"

"Yes" Ann answered. "Can I help you?"

"Commodore Leonard here, Admiralty, we have a job for you."

Harris shouted, "PARKER."

END

Lightning Source UK Ltd.
Milton Keynes UK
UKOW04f0736301013

220024UK00001B/10/P